The African Origins of UFOs

ANTHONY JOSEPH is a poet, musician and lecturer. He was born in Trinidad, moving to the UK in 1989. He is the author of two poetry collections: *Desafinado* (1994) and *Teragaton* (1997). In 2004 he was selected by the Arts Council of England for the historic 'Great Day' photo as one of fifty Black and Asian writers who have made major contributions to contemporary British literature. In 2005 he was the British Council's first Poet in residence at California State University, Los Angeles. As a spoken word artist he has performed internationally, including The Chicago Humanities Festival, Festa International De La Literatura, Barcelona, Spain, UCLA, Howard University, Washington and London's Queen Elizabeth Hall. He has taught creative writing at London Metropolitan University, University of Surrey, Roehampton and currently lectures at South Thames College, London.

Also by Anthony Joseph

Desafinado (Poison Engine Press, 1994)
Teragaton (Poison Engine Press, 1997)
Liquid Textology CD (Poison Engine Press, 2005)

The African Origins of UFOs

ANTHONY JOSEPH

Introduction by Lauri Ramey
Illustrations by infinite livez

SALT

CAMBRIDGE

PUBLISHED BY SALT PUBLISHING
PO Box 937, Great Wilbraham, Cambridge PDO CB1 5JX United Kingdom

First published 2006

Printed and bound in the United Kingdom by Lightning Source

Typeset in Swift 9.5 / 13

ISBN-13 978 1 84771 272 4 paperback
ISBN-10 1 84771 272 9 paperback

SP

1 3 5 7 9 8 6 4 2

for Meena ïerè and Louise

Contents

Acknowledgements

Thanks to my wife Louise for her infinite love and support, to my daughter Meena ïerè, my hummingbird.

To my family in Trinidad; my father, who inspired much of this work, my brother, sisters and Auntie Ursula, who calls. And to my mother-in-law Dawn Lewis.

Special thanks to Lauri Ramey for her generous energy and guidance and for writing an introduction that explains more than I ever could. To infinite livez for his fantastic illustrations. To Kamau Brathwaite, Wilson Harris, Linton Kwesi Johnson and Nathaniel Mackey for their encouragement/s and inspiration.

To Jonathan Barker, Sarah Frankland, Molly Michal and Andy Mackay at the British Council UK & US. Thanks to Melanie Abrahams at renaissance one. To Sylvia Gaspardo-Moro and Charles Ray in Los Angeles, Ardella Jones at South Thames College and to Chris and Jen Hamilton-Emery at Salt for their spirit and commitment. They let me do my thing. Thanks to Tom Chivers for the business and to my fellow poets/writers in the UK and abroad, esp. Roger Robinson, Jacob Sam La Rose, Malika Booker, Charlie Dark, Karen McCarthy, Vanessa Richards, Khefri Riley, T'kalla and James Oscar. I stole vibe from them all at some time.

Thanks to Darren Lewis, Kemal Mulbocus, Martin 'Soca' La Borde, Roderick and Wendy Chasseau, Romain Rabier, Samantha Choudhury. Much love & gratitude to my brothers in the Spasm Band: Andrew John, Colin Webster, Yinka and Paul Zimmerman—dey leggo de lion!

Excerpts from this work have appeared in *Dark Matter: A Century of Speculative Fiction from the African Diaspora*, ed. Sheree Thomas (New York: Warner Books, 2000)

And in the literary journal *Hambone* #18, ed. Nathaniel Mackey California, 2006.

Introduction
by Lauri Ramey

Based on his two poetry collections—*Desafinado* (1993) and *Teragaton* (1997)—Anthony Joseph has developed an international reputation for combining the formal innovations of modern and post-modern avant-gardism with African diasporic practices. He is known for the frequent use of neologisms, a preponderance of conceptual abstractions, surreal imagery, references to folktales and other genres associated with magic realism, settings that are both futuristic and primeval, signifying and complex representations of character and identity, dexterous verbal riffs on the musical traditions of soca, calypso, reggae and jazz, and a kaleidoscopic array of dictions, registers and cultural reference points. Joseph has laboured with brilliant ingenuity to employ his syncopated, polysemic and polyphonic poetics for purposes of gut-bucket funky storytelling in his long-awaited first novel *The African Origins of UFOs*.

In *The African Origins of UFOs*, Joseph exploits and explores his central conception by imagining a diasporic wave extending into the future, but whose purpose is to reverse migration—to achieve a return to the Africa of pre-slavery history. Joseph has created a metaphorical space where former slaves have travelled to the future in order to arrive at a spiritual and physical 'home' located in a world in the past that has ceased to exist. By starting with this ingenious cognitive blend, Joseph employs a syncretic, diasporic and highly innovative blend of genres and styles. He demonstrates the way in which the African diaspora serves as the subject, inspiration, and rationale for the innovative use of form, whilst experimental traditions enable him to show the diaspora in a fresh light. One of the major formal and narrative goals of this novel is to illuminate the history of the African diaspora by retro-constructing a creation myth. By so doing, Joseph portrays the profound longing and search for home—and the ability to meaningfully regenerate their heritage—amongst people who have uniquely preserved their culture in exile.

This novel also represents a writer's aesthetic challenge to maintain his poetic roots, using the rhythms, images, pauses and intuitive leaps of verse to generate an exploratory narrative. There is a central 'plot' to *The African Origins of UFOs*, but it is a poet's sense of story, identity, perspective and sequence. It would be a mistake to distil the essence of this novel to characterisation and plot arc. Its structure, as shown, is both intricate and compressed. Characters are sketched by broad strokes that are at times reminiscent of Ishmael Reed's use of historical caricature. Events take place on multiple, and sometimes indeterminate, physical and psychological planes.

This is a novel of palimpsestic eras and settings, with a densely interwoven circular structure comprised of poetic fragments, dialogues, and blocks of sentences, which Joseph compares to the interweaving of his grandmother's braids. It is a poet's prose that Joseph refers to as 'liquid text fiction', combining lyric poetic rhythms and epic poetry ambitions with science fiction, Caribbean and African myths, and jazz.

In order to create 'the metaphysics of another world', the text is divided into twenty-four chapters. According to Joseph, 'This structure was inspired by the work of Dr Timothy Leary, who believed that human consciousness evolved through twenty-four evolutionary niches of three levels each, from birth to death, from stasis to stasis, from water to land to space to panspermic dust'.

Joseph found another source of structural and conceptual influence in Ornette Coleman's aesthetic philosophy of 'Harmolodics', which aims to create a seamless blend where all meaning is equal in the art object, and no element is hierarchically fore-grounded. This vision is similar to the Marxist egalitarianism of L=A=N=G=U=A=G=E poetry (a 1980s inheritor of Dada and other international movements of modernist experimentation) which also has impacted Joseph's style. In *The African Origins of UFOs*, the non-linear narrative threads and an amalgam of *personae*—which are both individuated and inevitably exemplars of a culture—seem to float in a futuristic and primordial simultaneity and equivalence of signification. Voices collude and collide, the past reflects the future, the future mirrors the past, and the present resonates across boundaries of time and space.

In keeping with Leary's philosophy, the twenty-four chapters are divided into three sections of eight chapters apiece. However—consistent with Coleman's theory of Harmolodics—the narrative design is cyclical and horizontal, moving as a network of parts rather than a vertical progression of events and actions leading towards resolution or revelation. The movement of the chapters is fugue-like instead of following Leary's strict order of the development of consciousness. The metaphorical cycle of twenty-four elements reflects a compressed vision of the self-regenerating lifespan of a culture—what Mircea Eliade refers to as the auroral beginnings inherent in myth—and suggests other literary representations of twenty-four hour time spans, including Leopold Bloom's archetypal odyssey.

Each section pairs a spatial and temporal location, which operates structurally as a built-in anti-map for unanchored travel in time and space. These dislocations and relocations are piloted by means of wildly syncretic and

frequently surreal imagery consisting of creative metaphorical blends, as discussed by Mark Turner and others: that is,
where source and target domains cannot logically coexist
except cognitively as 'blended spaces' in the literary text.
The first section is set in space in the future, the second
section on land in the present, and the third in water in the
past. To further complicate these 'systems within systems',
three different chapter headings reappear in all three
sections, though with differing subtitles, in a highly math-
ematical set of fractal forms.

The chapter headings called 'Kunu Supia' generally
represent space and the future. The 'Journal of a return to a
floating island' chapters generally represent land and the
present. The chapters called 'The genetic memory of ancient
Ïerè' generally represent water and the past. This pattern of
repetition and return creates movement that is simultane-
ously and alternately integrated, progressive and regressive.
Realms of existence—where intersection is metaphysically
impossible—are continuously juxtaposed and cross-mapped,
as if in some magical dimension or medium. Although
there are echoes or bleed-throughs, which take place mainly
through the narrator's drug-induced genetic flashbacks, one
time and place serves as each section's dominant 'ground'.
These fixed locations also dictate a point of quasi-orientation
for the mystically disembodied narrator, who appears to
float detached from Cartesian physics.

The novel's genesis lay in a story that Joseph found in a guidebook to Trinidad. An African called Daaga was captured by the British and conscripted into the British West India Army then stationed at St Joseph, Trinidad. He repeatedly said that he would return to Africa and take his people with him. One day in 1837, Daaga set fire to the barracks, and 'they set off to walk back to Africa'. Joseph was mesmerized by the strength of will that led to a man's determination to walk home across the elements. He imagined that Daaga and his companions travelled by spacecraft to a mythical Africa, and 'I then saw their journey as a metaphor for black people trying to find their roots'. That tale was the means by which Joseph decided that the genre of *The African Origins of UFOs* would be science fiction, but of a highly lyrical type that would enable him to explore questions of biological determinism and genetic memory. This supple genre could embrace such disparate components as satire, surrealism, Trinidadian folklore, DNA/RNA research, and the science of planet construction, to name a few.

The novel's first section—set in space in the future—is largely based in Toucan Bay, a replica of a Caribbean seaside town on the planet Kunu Supia in the year 3053. Its residents are of Ïerèan ancestry—in legend, Ïerè was the name given by the Meso-Indians to Trinidad, meaning 'land of the hummingbird'. The central premise is that Trinidad was destroyed by floods in the 30th century. Survivors migrated to Kunu Supia, where they essentially reproduced a Caribbean view of the American 'wild west'—complete with a brothel/bar called Houdini's Hideaway—in this carnivalesque outpost. By depicting Caribbean culture in space, Joseph creates a metaphorical and sometimes parodic representation of the diaspora, and of the resiliency of Black culture.

On Kunu Supia, geological processes have created a climate where only the darkest skinned humans can survive, with synthetic melanin as the contraband drug of the day. The feared pusher, Joe Sambucus Nigra, has ventured into the desert to bring back the high grade melanin desperately needed by the lighter skinned Kunu Supians. His many enemies await his return to Toucan Bay, including the assassin Bo Nuggy, Joe Sam's arch nemesis. This section's diction is the most formally innovative of the novel and reflects Joseph's vision of a cool post-apocalyptic Caribbean swagger of affect and sway of body. The hallucinatory quality of the language partially reflects the drug-induced flashbacks of the narrator, in which he relives events stored in his 'secret underlung', or the cultural history inscribed within his body. The narrative is distributed, with fragments of stories told by the narrator's ancestors, who describe an ancient Ïerè now destroyed. Other characters materialise in these 'soul cage' interludes, reappearing at intervals, and mediate the reader's voyages between Kunu Supia and the former Trinidad. Ultimately, past, present and future coalesce, culminating at the end of the novel in the integration of the elements of space, land and water, and enabling an impossible means of connecting the future with the past via the present.

The second section—'Journal of a return to a floating island'—takes place on land in the present. It refers to the state of permanent liminality in which the culture and geography of Trinidad now exist. In an allusion to Aimé Césaire's *Cahier d'un retour au pays natal*, the eight chapters comprise genetic flashbacks that form meditations on 'exile, return, and the futile search for the self one leaves behind'. Joseph conceives of these portraits as 'intimate travelogues, snapshots and sound paintings' made when 'going "home" for holiday'. This is a return to an island that can only exist 'in the ocean of memory, a contradictory place that is at once natal and dislocated. A space that changes forever once you leave it'. This section exemplifies the insistence and inescapability of the present tense, and the futility of trying to capture a past that is inaccessible— except, perhaps, through art.

Section three, 'The genetic memory of ancient Ïerè', is a series of creation myths set in water in the past. The eight chapters are infused with a sense of nostalgia, and the desire to reanimate the spirit and substance of Caribbean magic, myths, fables and rituals that have evolved into residual and vestigial memories. The only possible resolution to the dilemma proposed by this section—without giving away the novel's inspired conclusion—is to 'set off to walk back to Africa'.

Joseph's identity as a product of Trinidad's cross-cultural mixture—with its rich assortment of languages and heritages—undoubtedly has inspired the plethora of voices, dictions and registers that emanate from *The African Origins of UFOs*. Carnival, calypso and East Indian Trinidadian culture all add to the *callaloo* and its attendant sense of freedom that flavour Joseph's writing. In addition to the unmistakably Caribbean character of this book, African diasporic traditions abound: emphasis on family and cultural inheritance, accompanied by a sense of its dispossession; effort to create one's own functional world in the face of migration, joined to a strong belief in integrating the individual with a sustaining community; and cultural, psychological, and linguistic alienation from one's roots, along with a desire and need for sustained contact with deceased elders as spirit guides. Joseph's state of migration from Trinidad—a place where he can never again fully belong, but which is a central theme and source of his creative material—is the foundation of his identity as an artist.

Colonialism, migration, dislocation, psychological arrival and repatriation collide in Joseph's novel. In trying to find past and present exemplars who examined related terrain, Joseph found precursors in artists, writers, musicians, philosophers, and cultural critics associated with formal experimentation and counter-cultural practices, including Amiri Baraka, Ted Joans, Kamau Brathwaite, Wilson Harris, Léopold Sédar Senghor, Nathaniel Mackey, The Mighty Sparrow, Thelonius Monk, Miles Davis, John Coltrane, Ornette Coleman and Aimé Césaire. In blazing his own trail in such an illustrious community of role models, Joseph has displayed the talent and originality to join this pantheon of aesthetic originators. The brilliantly original achievement of *The African Origins of UFOs* is to use the novel form to decenter and reconceptualise identity, examine artistic connections across metaphysical boundaries with others who engaged in exploratory practices, and interrogate language as a system of discourse—but in a fresh and unique contemporary voice. Following on from such esteemed Caribbean forebears as Brathwaite and Harris, Anthony Joseph's first novel addresses the challenges of self-representation in a post-postcolonial world, and makes a major and unforgettable contribution to a new tradition of future fiction classics.

LAURI RAMEY, PHD
Director, Center for Contemporary Poetry and Poetics
California State University, Los Angeles

The African Origins of UFOs

1

Kneedeepinditchdiggerniggersweat

His voice had the deep burrr of a man who kept fishhooks in his beard. So I put on my white muslin jumpsuit, slid sleeves and levers tight, pulled my hair shut with Sirian beeswax and en-route superterranean to Toucan Bay via Antimatic Congo Pump I met Cain waiting with the contraband: 8 grams of uncut Ceboletta X.[1] And while Cain stroked a reefer the size of Mozambique rolled in a roti skin, I held my head wide open for the suck with a nasal>oral siphon and was so oiled and eager for Joe Sam's return to Houdini's' that night that I sped there, down near the jetty where fishgutfunk fumed furiously and found

3

copious peoples rubbing belly to back, hacking heels—knee deep in ditchdiggerniggersweat!

That naked island funk was steady lickin' hips with polyrhythmic thunderclaps! Does the Berta butt boogie? Do bump hips? Flip'n spin'n bop'n finger pop'n/subaquantum bass lines pumping pure people-riddim funk like snake rubber twisting in aluminium bucket, reverberating 'round the frolic house with a heavy heartbeat, causing black to buck and shiver—

WOOEEE! WOOEEE!—

The very groove caused coons to stumble loose and slide on Saturnalian pomade until their conks collapsed. The sound possessed more swing than bachelor galvanise in hurricane, more sting than jab-jab whip, more bone than gravedigger boots and more soul than African trumpet bone. It was that pure emotive speed that once improvised harmolodic funk to Buddy Bolden's punk jazz on the banks of Lake Pontchartrain, double bass still reverberating through space-time like long lost Afronauts on orbiting saxophones. And the solid sound did shook Spiritual Baptist shacks with rhythm, till the Sankey hymns they sung became cryptic mantras that slid like secrets through water.

Up the varnished teak banister, ever afrodizziac in Indian red, with her high sepia 'fro, far east eyes and blood black morello lips borrowed from a jealous mirror,

Madame Sweetbum peeps then leans back on her arse for
support. Puffin' good genk and inspecting vinyl imprints in
dry blue light, releasing slap after slap of the raw boned
and ancient Afrolypso she kept in titanium sleeves —
sacred 45s so sharp rip slippers off feet till steam hisses
from her radiogram. Madame Sweetbum had negroes
wringing brine! Her hi-hat kickin' fat back an' brass,
swingin' — black be boogiefull, black be slick, cryptic
hustlers an' assorted Cyberpimps in stingy brim fedoras,
scissor-tongued vipers in snakeskin brogues, in pleated
pollywool zoot suits with sawed off buckshots in their
lapels. Nubile Supian woman throwing waist like whip-
snake, slip slide/rabid-eyed by stiff crotched coons in erec-
tion boots, leaning at the bar boppin' bulbous foreheads
an' burnin' for flesh.

Meanwhile, Mokotux Charlie climbed the stairs like a
caliper with his clipboard, mop and megaphone. The old
bush coolie ran the place with the rep n'grace of a
gambler's tears. Molasses black with a face like an
unfinished woodcarving, tight brown suit, cockroach killer
boots, white handle razor behind an ear for peeling more
than toe corns and a voice that suggested a rusty trachea.
Charlie liked to grin in that old island pimp style, revealing
ten teeth brown from fifty-five years of Trini pepper, chewing nush and home-rolled cigars. He also ran severe
érotique noir upstairs where the rooms smelled like dried

pussy, where cum crusted face rags lay under the beds, where the curtains drooped dank and butter greased while his ladies charged by the pound; your weight plus theirs in cash!

Charlie hummed as he shovelled spum from teledildonic booths and wiped his pros with paraffin. Prime pros with lineage through ancient ïere; pork-legged jamettes and melon swallowing domestic cleaner types with devious profiles, big bone dada mamas whose hips re-tuned bedsprings to the B flat of authentic colonial brothels. Some wore names like Yvette, Rose, Daphne and Gemma who'd just arrived on Kunu Supia from some floating island behind God's back and she would even let you lick her mastectomy scar.

But every time the front door swung grown negroes gaped, glass to lip, sippin'slow, peeping through booze for Joe. Say say,

"Joe mark to dead, reserve Brandy, salt biscuit, slice cheese!"

Joe Sam been gone ninety-nine and one half days. No one no where knew but some speculate, claim say he been seen hunting giant crustacea in the Kilgode desert, circumpolar roaming with genetic contraband/he sure to come back head hard with niggerknots—with a calabash fulla manjak bitumen between elbows. Soon's his shuttle land Kunu people go run down from the rainforest to scope Joe

in flesh. Assassins too, go be sharpening they tools, 'cause
all them know one thing for surety: Joe Sam
                                        doh
                                    eat   nice!

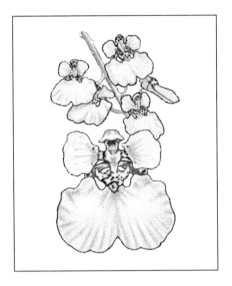

[1] Ceboletta: Dragon blood, spider lily, cocoa onion, Orhid Oncidium, *lagrimas de la virgin, Eleutherine Bulbosa (Iridaceae)*. Cocoa panyols in the valleys of Caura, ancient ïerè, worshipped this medicinal plant, nurtured and fed it, cared for it as a child, soaked the ground with blood and milk and planted it at the boundaries of their land. The conqueros used it as a vermifuge (infusion of the underground bulb) for menstrual pain and intestinal disorders. Known to cause genetic flashbacks (phenanthrene derivatives of unknown hallucinogenia). It is said to whistle at night.

2

JOURNAL OF A RETURN TO A FLOATING ISLAND

Malick

:: arrive in the early evening. red dusk shimmers in the
/trees/light sparks mosaics of diamond. climb down dirt
into the village and the dogs begin to bark. tantie selma at
her kitchen window. when she sees me sends her laughter
travelling first. then she comes, wiping her hands in her
dress/brisk, her slipper slapping.

embrace her/her full body.

my aunt selma she is older now. her beard gone grey, as her
mother's did. her jowl fuller. her hands are wire veined. but
still she speaks with the tone of small birds, of parakeets,

or yellow corn birds. it is a voice reserved for an only daughter. light blows through her house like wind through a sieve, shaking dust from two frayed albums of old photographs under her corrugated coffee table. selma at twenty-one is a framed studio portrait hung on the wall, beautyfull bust of the princess in pink sleeveless dress and pearls the year she married.

now deep bush hugs the hill her shelter rest on. and sugarcane grows wild beside her latrine. hand hemmed curtains bloom heat through both rooms dim with humid lumber. condensed milk, burnt garlic and cinnamon. the floor kept swept of red ants, brown sugar. the wind chime loose. she brings coffee, make we speak, let night come down like silk cotton breeze.

well all is hills around this valley and bush. the seeping pulse of dusk on galvanize and tungsten white light from wooden verandas, the blues and mellow greens of these windswept, pastel painted shacks of my cousins, old aunts and their great grand nephews, chickens asleep on the guava tree. black back crapaud still weeping in the gullies.

even my father's bachelor shack is a ridge further up the mountain. when i hear his voice it is singing, and his boot spittin' dirt, coming up the track, bracing on his sister selma's pillar posts/ already drunk from drinking at work.

> *embrace him . .*
>> *his whole self*

his grin still charms seams cut in crimpelene,

>> *. . with his arms strung down . .*

his neck still smells of tobacco and coal tar soap.

his beard still drips whisky, wild meat, raw egg.

> *remove his cap and kiss his baldplate tenderly.*

my father takes his coffee black with sugar and a cigarette. then we all sit under moonlight in selma's sloping yard, as her laughter goes tumbling round the valley. my father says,

"ah puttin' down some tiles for a 'oman up mt hololo — and jus'so tonight she open a bottle a scotch, man in two-twos i finish de wuk! now she say she may have more wuk for me."

Buddha

my father has four flags planted at the side of his house.
secret colours.
he would not name them.
he say he been to china, see buddha sit on a throne,
he say he in a group looking up: at buddha.
he say buddha take a chillum from his waistband, lit it
    and suckt it.
then the pipe pass around everyone in the circle.
      buddha call—"al—bot!"
an' albert had to pass between guards on both sides had
    swords
    and kneel down.
an' buddha put a bead necklace round his neck and say,
    "i give you gift, you give no one."
he say in the spirit world everything have life,
    he say he speaks to trees and animals,
say he seen jumbie with caduceus upon dem head.
say he been to the bottom of the sea/been standing on the
    guinea coast
and two african man come out of the sea and say,
    "ai you, you eh see you naked?"
and they took him by both hands and into the water
    and washed him.
then give him a gown—half yellow half brown—an' one say
    "let this be your shield, this word be your sword"
and with this they transferred secret syllables to his ear.
he say then one take a dagger
    an' chook 'im in he waist/but the blade
would not penetrate the gown. he say,
    "boy sometimes i jus' drink two guinness,

go kick back an' meditate. when I ketch myself i find myself
in ethiopia someway."
and then he shows me the necklace
    between his shirt.
my father stands, fixes his brim—pours cold coffee dripping
    in the calabash root
and leaves/uphill to bathe
in cold water
but falls asleep face down in his bachelor bed, still in his
    string vest,
drawers and argyle socks, cradling a bottle of duty free rum

and the sea   blows up   from the horizon

3

The Thunderstone

She called them Thunderstones because they fell from the sky. May spirits build nests in her beard.

She would find them in the savannah on her way back from the market or in the moist dirt of her garden while clipping hibiscus or picking limes for her dry season menopause. They were smooth, perfect petals of secret black stone; cool against the face, warm and natural to the palm. Somehow she knew them from the eggs of ancient bones and would test them with candle and thread; that did not burn, the stone, ever fell, or the world would end.[1]

: wipe them with the hem of your dress and place them in
intimate spaces.

She would press them in her palms when he broke her
bare. And when he cussed, she would pray. Yet these stones
she kept. One in every sack of woe. She would say,
   "See God face? If you see God face you dead."
And would place a seamless stone between her hymn book
and her soft-candle heart. One for the old man's gun draw,
one for her sequinned purse, one beside the wardrobe door,
between her bible and goblet of croton. One in black jacket
pocket for good luck, lost among camphor and nylon, one
to steady doily in tropic gusts.
   She kept them as others did the eyes of serpents and
gave them as gifts as others gave seeds and fetishes. These
stones were not for skimming streams or scrubbing pots;
was wisdom she brought with her from the sea. Indeed,
some kept scars from rolling under islands.
   And once she told me,
   "When God dig, dirt to make man was black, deeper 'e
go then, whiter it get."
   As she bent, ripping weeds from round her marigold,
spider lily, poinsettia

                    (euphorbia pulcherrima, fire plant, painted leaf)

                          ∽

So when the census man came counting me one was first
to say,

"Me is nigger sa', negro."

But my grandmother she put a soft palm to my shoulder
and smiled—

"No, oh no, we mixed essence please, beetle meat, roast
scorpion, we pure cocoa panyol, is Spanish, African, Chinee
and Amerindian."

Her blood knit hammocks across the Gulf of Paria.

She must have known they were meteorite particles.
Those stones, flung far from Siderite mines—interstellar
souvenirs of biological dust. She came walking over the
mountain, across the savannah with a jute sack a yam and
green banana on her head. Cocoa onion, crown of thorns.

(*Euphorbia splendens*. And its toxic sap.)

∼

Her dress came first, dancing before her with the trade
winds. She had walked along precipes and riverless bridges
from Caura village through the northern range and
upward sacred mountains.

Down El Tucuche,

through La Canoa,

Mt Hololo, Susconusco,

Pipiol,

Bourg Malatrese,
via La Pastora, Cantaro and Caura valley.

As a girl in old Caura, she rode mules through Poopa Lezama's plantation bush to pick wild coffee. She flushed the hog pen and fed the butterflies, she cracked corn for the hens, cassava for pone. Farine for dough.

Is just so one day a plane would whine and dive. She saw it plummet for the hills and she ran to shiver hid between zebafanm bush an banana leaf, when Cipriani plane crash in El Chiquero that Sunday morn. She watched the machine fail and fall, how smoke rip out like kite tail, and then the sound would echo in the jungle.

And by the time we saw her walk
                                through Aranguez savannah,
she carried three small children in her armpit and a wreath of miscarriage lavender.

~

He was a lean and sombre carpenter when she met him. Augustus, a Bajan: his grinning eye reserved for chasing scotch with pepper pork on Christmas morning. He often ate egg bread and rode an old iron Humber cycle through rugged island terrain, selling teak swizzle sticks and foot-stools. He built latrines and cedar commodes, working from sweat till dawn 'cause he was ambitious. Is so he bought three acres of untamed earth, this floating island east, at the edge of Aranguez savannah.

Is so one day he go build one shack, to keep his tools and work shoes. Same one to shelter when it rain and rainfly come up from the mist, and sandfly start bite, and scarlet Ibis stood knuckle deep in the flooded field. And when he laid his foundation stone, all round the settlement was zebapip bush and fever grass. And mongoose sucking snake through bamboo.

There were lush fields of rugged earth further east, paddy farms and cabbage yards to the south, cat snake in strange fruit tangling the land with vine. Augustus was patient; he built a house around them like clothes sewn on to the body. He fed her children and built her cupboards to keep, money for cloth and new shoes. He even send she go dentist to fix she mouth.

But upstairs the old tobacco house on Champs Fleur hill he ran illegal liquor rooms where pros and their patrons would congregate to blow gage and sip bush rum, spill dice and slam aces high.

"O gorm, 'gustus left home since foreday Friday mornin'."

She wrings her hands and prays, standing in the kitchen looking out to the field. And that Sunday, just past dusk, she leaves home to walk a mile an' a half up Champs

Fleur hill. From here the eye extends to the southern horizon, to the Caroni canefields, to starlit spirals of smoke from molasses refineries. But she has not come for the view; she weaves a trail of tears. And the cool night wind speaks shivers in her bosom. And yet she notices that there are more stars than sky, dust of the moon, the sun still shining through rock. Thunderstone falling.

High pitched calypso exfoliates the night . . .

Caroline and Josephine making more than fifty
And I'm sure without any doubt they could be my granny
Still they walking 'bout at night with they face like Jack Palance
Go to France! Step aside and give your daughters a chance.

~

She climbs the wooden stairs, each step slowly.
Her dress is homegrown green, the hems are bruised. Her pomade balm is copranut oil; her head is a pillowcase of blues. She searches the crowded room to find him, past the jacket men and the wasp waist saga boys from town, the bagatelle jammetes and their barrackyard laughter. Augustus, chasing gin with lime, spit and shine, his sawdust jaw, his grind like teak, each step he groove make the floorboards creak. There he stands at the bar . . . grinning still,
when she touched him.

¹ Tell you about rubies and other precious stones I found in the brook that runs through my natal land. A river from a swerving hedge of foliage gushes. In it I glimpse a shining something/milk snake skin—but a calabash gourd washed smooth by the water or a serpents eye preserved by the bamboo's rind. A hollow chamber. I disheveled its crust. Inside was an onyx bone thunderstone of the genus she kept in her purse.

And when the river speaks I listen. Deep runs the history of this river through this floating island. Space exists where we thought mattered. The earth is indeed hollow, not solid as was thought. The inhabitants of the inner sanctum are rust colored red from the dust of porous stones.

The smooth black stone seemed to possess an eye that could trace my bloods' trajectory. But a shout sent me sprawling swift through the vortex, that I still clutched the stone, I would've been swept through the dragon's mouth if not.

Geometric blue within
A yellowcore, for spiritduality.
Red creeps in from the side.
Green light or light green and grey
Splits the sky in two

Lake top a plateau. Wide. Blooming trees and up this hill is a lagoon of blood red water. Each glimpse between light reveals surrealist objects in the water: a headless Seahorse, la belle firefly skeleton, an Iguana out of its skin's proportion bloated pale green afloat on its side. Ravine eel and river weed, triple headed catsnake and leaves of eyes.

I see her run to come up the hillside and beg her be careful. 'cause when I looked down all I could see saw no incline, just a steep drop, a plummet to stone and the tumble down seemed crocus bound. When we stand there looking out through the moist haze she says,
        "I'm bleeding all over."
Now every room smells of lavender.

Suddenly the sky blinks and the ship bears down like a metal rag. And when it hits it breaks and people rush to keep its cryptic parts, its twisted levers, osidium bolts and brutal discs etched with vistas of Caribbean seascapes. Peninsulas and bays. Each fragment authentic, but the ruins contain no one alive. The captain abdicated and is found fifty miles away. A Methodist spire cracks and falls across the street. One man try hop and duck but capsize an' broke his arsebone. The bar was completely destroyed. Many died. Most were crushed and mangled by spinning metal as the ship tumbled down the precipice. Below the bay spread majestic lips of sand, and the jungle vibrated green and blue in multiple frequencies. The pilot snarled as he gripped the wheel, stiff teeth grit, in the blazing cockpit. But he let go no sound as he fell from the sky.

4

Killer Joe

Si dieu les rendait noirs
il doit signifier quelque chose

Joe Sam was so bad even catfish shaved to meet him: a man so fierce he wore his boots in-side-out. African space-boots, Nigerians used them for terraforming; Joe Sam used his to kick afro saxons and smuggled his black butter irregardless. Bad like crab an' spoken of with contempt in multiple dialects of intergalactic niggaspeak, banned from six floating isles for ultraviolence, subversive texts and possession of genetic contraband, upright and devious with a stare that saw through bones—his instantaneous cuss was so cantankerous it would cause concussions!

So gifted in the throat with a Baptist minister's grimy tone, his aural pyrotechnics would hypnotise negroes. A callous, transgalactic pusherman, suave an' so slick with a flick he filled veins stiff with liquid essence; supplying pale-folk and tourists with prime niggum vitae. He drove a chrome Mesakin Congo Pump with antimatic injection. Ever dapper in devious strides and astro-camouflage dashikis, Joe Sam's hustle was the cusp of voodoo funk technology: bootleg melanin to keep pale niggers ticking on Kunu Supia!

Joe swore lineage to Ïerèan ancestors who were *rois* and *dauphins* in secret slave militias, belly marinated with the bile of cocksmen and killers from Corbeau Town to Cuttyville junction. Men with wooden carbuncles and full heads of hair, who shaved with cutlass blades. Copasetic men who would nyam pigfat, mandrake root and forceripe tamarind for breakfast then buck waist and break fast an' spit revolutionary spunk from a radius of 360°. Coming from the genus of mythical beasts from back in old Ïeré when stickfighthers still ruled the ancient barrackyards; hill-born soldiers with cast iron gorgon organs and *bois* dipped in asafoetida sulphate, underarm renk with rancid paraffin copper.

∼

Saliva trickles
from the lisp of a twelve fingered manchild tugging a kite
in Aranguez savannah/ with a razor bladed tail to cut and
send other kites over the Samaan trees then run home
watch: Electric Company, Love American Style, Carnabas
Bollins and Puffin' Stuff, Voyage to the bottom of the Sea—
they had no broughtupsy—would suck pus an hit big man
mad bullpistle then rub stinging nettle on dey prick, would
hunt snakes and whip lizards in half against orange trees
with masonry twine. Soulman pusherman skank to Mikey
Dread, bust carbide and smoke tampi, bust cow face with
broomstick, hog head with tree trunk, looting the city
while the revolution blazed!

Grow dread: upset the ol'lady.

Who convinced Gallstones Grandfather Buckmouth
that drinking lil'boy urine would cure his cataract but then
put mentholated spirit in the old man's hibiscus tea and
grew up to be legends with monikers as sublime as: Dr Rat,
Cutouter, Gooter, Siparia Scipio, Catpiss Pepper. Whatever
happened to Newland Blake? Mitagau? Or anyone a dem
rubber wristed *bois* swingers with hollow scars stolen from
the gayelle.

Big strong cocoa-prick man like Joe Sam so could sit in
a hot funky latrine, in a cane cutter shirt, sun cutting
through galvanise like Michael X pelting chop and smoke
a basiment of caustic ses and sip flour-porridge. Bus' toe

bounce steppers who had afros since the 1940s and would catch bullets there—much hair. Sharpboned jaw box go crack cocoa pod and coconut, bust tamboo bamboo, strip cane, shake skulls and squeeze out butterwax, break man back with 2 × 4 pine, restore blacknuss, plot guerrilla ballistics, peel back bullshit, stew black justice, high browed on JuJu metaphysics, sip breast milk, cow milk, duck egg and oyster, grow gut and full Pharaoh Sanders beard 'til it grew grey and long so would wrap around standpipes and Baptist flagpoles. But by then coming down from hill to town to tumble in teargas became impractical, and bad for bunions. Soon Swamp Dogg sang for them on Sunday morning as they reclined on verandas sipping rum and lime, body weak from revolution.

But Joe Sam appeared impervious to age. Ever eager to rangle/eager to bone, say say he wood like child foot how he induced spontaneous coitus in Bahama mamas and let off spum in spasms. Many men who swung grievance would shiver and cringe like ti marie leaf and surrender their deepest compunctions. When Joe grew rage he flashed his grandfather's blade, a black cold iron machete with a luminous brink; a suave blade steeped in the graves of ancients and passed over each generation. Joe Sam been grinnin' this same blade since long before the firearm ban. Who vex blush, who rush loss.

Smith was beaten.

Sharkos, like a snake. With the planass side.

Johnny Gren-Greng had his nose split with a slap
Chando got bust from arsehole to elbow.

Diba the barber tried flex; he owed Joe for four or more
vials of rare Touareg melanin. Ever broke when Joe call cash
yet always busy 'cause dada head sprouts like liquid text in
this sunpower. When Joe came to measure his grave
he was eating a mango. Diba gargled, he gulped: two vials
and hobbled to hide behind his leatherette swivel/eh heh?
—Joe caught him quick 'neat the talcum and splayed his
blade crisp on the terrazzo floor. Diba then, a rugged ol'
felon, one eye Abobo and citrus pungent drunk, swung a
razor that almost bust Joe gluck, but Joe jus' shift an'
sweetly sliced the barber from ear to jowl with his Gilpin
cutlass tip!

The speed it shook Diba sober to the very marrow and
he dropped his knees and moaned,

"Oo gooosh, Joe? wait, wait, me eye burning in me head
like capsicum!"

Joe made him drink warm salted milk and senna then
shell his shit out for the vials like for grapes in mud. When
he succumb (poor Diba try but he couldn't find them all)
Joe up an' bust a cutlass slap that almost shut his heart
down. Diba grab a bottle of King Doris pomade and he
broke it to a blade against a counter side, but Joe Sam spun
an' kicked it out his hand then he root the blade tip in Dida

eye. Say say when Diba eye bus' he bawl like a cow, shivered
and coughed up smoke, and as he fell he cried—
    "Coule sang coule moen sang coule . . ."
Who saw say he shot a stale yellow spunk that perforated
his barber's apron and lamp oil slid from his gaping wound.

∾

Joe been gone ninety-nine and one half days. Some speculate he been hunting giant crustacea in the Kilgode
desert/ some claim him in the south Kunu delta hustlin'
genetic contraband an' bound to come back head hard
with niggerknots, with a calabash fulla manjak bitumen
between elbows. He sharpened his toes.
    Joe Sam go deep south of the desert, past the devil's
wood yard and the mud volcanoes, across the great salt
dunes to the Concosa canyons to deal illicit oil with the
ruggedest Abobos. Soon's Joe reach all crook and spook and
ditchdigger would scamper out from under shale stone like
lizard, to sell their essence cheap. Some even tried to ply
the great man with rubber for hash/lamp oil for butter, dry
gin for government juice, molasses for melanin. But Joe
knew mouth from pussy and he kept them confused with
big money and fibre optic syringes. Say say is so Joe built a
stack of enemies.

5

Town

what sprouts now from these streets
where once familiar shadows strolled?

east:

long walking city streets for spices to build aromatic suit-
cases. herbal fetishes. across prince and down charlotte,
george and henry. strolling through the dry soul west of
the dry river for sandals and sugar cane brandy. for
nutmeg, smoked herring, mauby bark, anise seed, obie
seed, tonka bean, creole cocoa, wild indian thyme, red
lavender, kananga water, camphor seed and navel oranges,
ripe water melons in heaps on the crocus bound pavement,

plus a chaos of scents—bay rum, ammonia, stewed chicken
—but then, from across the street past a rum shop comes
some crooked mouth—

"ai—yankee yankee! gimma dollar nah, gimma dollar
nah"

in woodford square: arid grass gruff, poorfolk asleep in the
roots of old immortelles, and a steady draft of piss funk
ammonium blinks from the public toilets. the sun falls
across the bandstand and sprays a heat that heightens
every colour within the square. near the red iron gates, a
group of white headed baptists set up to testify, with
goblets and beads and asafoetida burning, chanting psalms
and the mother strong preach till her apron wet, still ringing bells in the buzzing heat. to the south, a swirl of tall
palms sway from the gardens of trinity cathedral, a gothic
spire, hallowed arches, a priest walks slowly from his pres-
bytery in a luminous white robe.

) town >

riot of noise and colour. revel rhythm speed and jumbie
bead. a ferment of light and sonic fever/ hot flesh rubs brisk
with flames of song down frederick street slick taxis pass by
booming dub and incense smoke, cocoa mango lily of the
valley kush kush musk / her hip swing too quick to capture
—senses drown in this human intensity. here we measure

time by temperature, distance by breath/like,
    "sister mamie, them heavy hips an' high heel leavin'
holes in me bitumen."
step light, dayblaze burning in the ground.

along henry street, pavement boutiques lean against fabric
store windows. hung on wire vines from the black felt
boards are hand crafted brass rings and bracelets, earrings
from the dolphinous fruit of the sandbox tree, polished
sandals cut from matelot leather, ladies handbags rinsed
from calabash gourds; each etched with intricate motifs
concealing hummingbirds in flight.

a one armed hustler lays his loot down on the street; ragged
old kaiso and brassorama albums salvaged from fire by a
fireman's flood. brother mudada, lord nelson, valentino,
black stalin, lord maestro; for five dollars each in water
warped cardboard sleeves.
    "take five for 20 red man, a have six weeks to live"
same time a cutlass hand hacks a water nut split for coco
jelly, come come the fresh 'n salt peanut man bumpin'
locks head, or the oyster vendor wiping his palms with
lime.

but saturday afternoon, in a broken room. first floor colonial verandas and dusty louvre blades. from the old fire

station overlooking st vincent street
air is moist with
immanence

.spirit come down from the steaming bush and lead me
across the gayelle.
show me by diagrams with chalk on the pitch pine floor, so
i can let my voice rise and fill the room.
you two mama! drum
come sit spirit, next to this drum.
and sunday night. my brother still saddened sits in the
backseat mournful and distant with his dread tied back.
she left this morning.
she walked down the hill and did not look back. he ran
after
but came back without her,
collapsed on my shoulder crying

thick black love

Gazette Paper: Notes from the National Archives

If from Africa we pass to the new world, the market of slaves, thoroughbred Congo—possession of a nose that might bob for black beetles against Christendom—was a mouth—dark and deep and odorous as the Grotto del Cane in Italy while the eye glared in a more than ordinary manner. The attitude of the man vied in elegance with the vulgo-immortalised/long ears and crop of curly wool the upper outline as complete as, negroland ever sent armed savages not less than one hundred and fifty in number, animated with the most deadly intentions and armed with the deadliest of all weapons.[1] Jules alias Fabo, about six feet six inches, has marks on his face and very black complexion, with utmost rigor but/ 3 a.m. Sunday morning made a rush upon the main guards and quarters of the old soldiers muskets set fire to the barracks that the sergeant major escaped through the back but without clothes and our dead in the woods, three having strangled their braces and the others hung and died of his wounds. At present there are not eight men of the regiment accounted for the chief however, a man of colossal stature, six feet six in height, nothing daunted, returned reloading his musket from a large quantity of loose powder and bullets which were carried in a foraging cap slung under his arm.[2]

1   The Bomb. The surprise or mystery song. A non-calypso rehearsed by a steelband especially for the Jourvert/ Carnival Monday morning 'Bomb' competition. The band practices secretly after midnight, often without sound, using fingers or pencils instead of pan-sticks. Pannists will not even discuss the tune amongst themselves and most will not have heard the whole tune, until the bomb is 'dropped' on unsuspecting masqueraders on Jourvert morning.

2   In 1956, the legendary steel pan innovator Capt. Anthony 'Tony' Williams (born 1930) of North Stars Steel Orchestra put wheels on the bass pans to aid maneuverability. According to steel pan legend, Williams needed a particular 'up in air' sound from the bass pans to play a tune called 'Puerto Rico Mambo'. Eventually metal frames and wheels were utilized by entire bands, enabling pannists to play multiple pans. Prior to this, steel drums were either balanced on seated players' knees or carried by straps around the neck.

6

Hummingbird

Witness this pure liquid text
                spun from fragments of genetic memory.
Earth long. Vintage Caribbean gold. Of ancient ïerè
before the flood.
Remember when cocoa panyol grease was as thick as
        earwax?
And dead eye jumbies hung like mannequins
by strands of cobwebbed sadness
over negroes brisk grinnin', lindy hoppin'
to naked island jazz
        in tenement discoteks,
busy rubbin' thigh to bone'n bonin' broko-foot mattress
        makers
in pumpenginejitneys.

'member when in seablast an' salty bars on the plaza
    marina
hairy toothed slum lizards washed their hands in
    turpentine?
And switched blades to bleed.
And pimps did bump all year but in February
They'd pawn their jewels for sailor mas or sequinned spears
              to hunt Nile crocodile
       on the sun bleached streets of old ïeré city.
Rem'ber when mama wrapt navel string in Bacano leaf
and buried it under
a guava tree?
And sealed the belly
with a knot.
And sealed the knot
with crushed insect bone.
When Al Green shivered then moaned, 'cause uncle Champ
                       was on the deck.
        Well was to see them spirit rise!
        from the steaming bush to dance.
And more cousins keep comin' over the hills with flambeau
    blazing
for babash rum
    and brown chicken rice.
Remember when scarfaced pan men carried machetes
under their fingernails and sharpened bones with
    quadraphonic steel? It was still tribe against tribe
    when the steelbands clasht—
and blood, bile, phlegm and rum
would run through alleys and gutters, through ravines
    steep with
pantywash and afterbirth tissue,

dragging trampled masks and broken headpieces, slits of
    glitter—
          to the river.
And now only the river remembers when
    Cariban Indian first cartographed this land
        and called her

                          ((((ïeré   ))))

7

Secret Underlung

But there were haters who grumbled at Joe's return. And in the brisk underbelly of night, savage native neck lockers crept in shadows with sharkbone daggers, in lurk for Joe arriving. They snuck and steupsed 'round Houdini's, peepin' neat the dank stairwells, grinding malice for Joe. To blow his soul. To bust
his secret underlung.

His modus upset some post-earth negroes who believed inner:disembodied:blacknuss and they bemoaned Joe for his black dada retrograde. They claimed that **black** as a concept of being was only ever relevant on Earth, and even then it was suspected as the mindset of a con that pat afros down and kept negroes terra bound to suffer/when we coulda been interplanetary from way back. Instead of the industrial revolution, we could've had niggers in space! They said black was dead. Black as in the tones of Nuyorican niggerpoets ranting militant in ancient days, earth long, living in cold water Brooklyn warehouse space, no food but Fanon, no cash but Jackson! Back then them rhetoric was hip and On-the-One 'cause subversive boots and dreader guerrillas were needed on the urban battlefields and word was sword, shield and dagger. Even ancient ïeré had gun in dashiki and afro intellects bust plenty police head with oratorical gas but not now we swimming in heaven.

With such consummate scripts these anti-essentialists wished to reverse polarities. But black people didn't want to hear that shit! 'cause in their folly these fools grew lame limbs and underneath and otherwise they appeared impervious to funk. The ONE would hit them in the chest like this <!> and they wouldn't understand it. Prone to pork they'd lick pigfat off the floor when no one was looking but they wouldn't understand it. Their ears would ring with trans-genetic texts and they wouldn't understand it. Drums would tumble with insecret textures and they wouldn't understand it.

And if they could they would eradicate Joe.

Or blow his soul or bust. His secret underlung.

But on this side of the Supian Sea, the most feared and ultraviolent spooks were the Abobos. Mix no matters. They were the mutant progeny of terraformers who churned in geothermal mines till sun bust their genome codes in the Kilgode desert and they and their kin became the pure *black dada annialismus* with eyes that shone like sunbeams through smooth onyx bone! Who put caduceus 'pon dem pineal gland, dem who deep black like coal pot bitumen from scalp to sole with skin the texture of calfskin leather. They wore crocus sack jumpsuits, jute! or raw kapok silk, they snuck devious with burnt steel sabres, dry ice blades; 'savage', 'inhuman'. They roamed grim retrotech cat-o-nine tails.

They wanted to hurt Joe. Real bad. To suck the marrow from his thigh bone. Firstly, for heresy. And too, with perilous envy of the slick ease with which Joe Sam rolled billfolds in Toucan Bay from Abobo oil he bootleg in the Kilgode desert. Until Joe came over the mountain, they spun that hustle tight and now they say how Joe Sam greed for niggergeneseed leave plenty Abobo to pine. Like magga wood. But Joe say he deals it upright and proper, never leave them dissatisfied. Aboboman insist still he needs be broke down + Diba was a dada to nine.

Two Abobo them was rappin' in a gully underneat Houdini's in their crude basilect:

"I hear Joe Sam kill twenty man with Idi Amin jawbone
—all was Spyro Gyra fans."

"Is so? Well Laro if yuh dead I go bury yuh clothes, but
me, I 'fraid. If Joe clap I feel I go duck. My lil' iron cyar ramp
with a man like he; a go get me eye bus' up, like Diba."

"Tha's good talk Bucky, let Penco give charge, 'cause
when Joe ketch rage 'e footey kill all a we!"

Kunu people clap foot an' hip shake on the hot so hot
was a rugged groove kickin' fat from Madame Sweetbum's
disco deck and a sea of arms rise up when the singer
chants,

Gyul you eh fraid you man go beat you?
I come out to play!
                    Me eh hah no man I tell yuh
I come out to play!

Dress hems be wailing—pollywool be sharp! Basspump
rattlin' through the floorboards/tot tots bouncing/liquor
flow an' throw, up runneth over. Kunu people love a jam an'
wine and spin 'pon heel and dingolay. But between beats
assassin agents of genetic piracy stalked the Hideaway like
jumbie for they beads. And hooded negros, leaning at the
bar sipping hot gin an' paraffin kept their brims shut—bad
eye burnin' knot in eyebrow scoping the swinging doors for
Joe Sam coming.

Bevies of hefty henchmen shuffled evil incognito near the entrance. Way they shift was conspicuous. Way they strummed their beards. Way they secret scalp with exotic hat and tap/pd odd rhythm like Monk. And whispered slick in undercuts reserved for lovers, plotting Joe's demise.

∾

Bo Nuggy

Bo Nuggy worked in the Jalo Ice Factory by day, by night he studied Spinoza. But unknown to many, Bo was also a felon for hire whose bulk alone would terrorise. Bo Nuggy gut big to bully goons for illicit brass in fibregrass alleys. Bo Nuggy big but he quick to whip lash with cape stiff an' cutlass blinking. Even so, Bo gulp shook when he considered Sambucus. 'Cause he remembered seeing Joe Sam muscle flex, knocking iron in a Spasm Band on Jourvert morning— quick to clap a man plus Joe Sam real smart. Earlier at the bar, Bo Nuggy talk gruff an' stutter,

"JoJoJoe jus' reach, an' a gogogoin'in 'e mudacont!" And everyone laughed and left him with the iron sweating in his palm.

"History is mine! A bound to mangle Joe Sam and sssseize all genetic contraband!"

Bo Nuggy wide like Samaan tree trunk, his gut swung low. His shaven skull bore scars and sketches of wounds. His grin never blinked. Broad nosed and bearded, Bo Nuggy ate raw duck egg and boiled hog at dawn/gut fulla dog rice, tripe and split pea soup, cow heel porridge, yam and red salted butter. Bo grew moss in the moist folds of his neck, smelled like turtle rot. He step with foot them wide like young jookin' board. And in private, Bo Nuggy would kneel—

"Oh Lawd, help me lose this weight."

But the lord wasn't listening.

Bo Nuggy descended from a brace of ancient ïeréan robbers who lived in hills above the lost city; dry river waterfall—where crapaud smoke your pipe if bad bush stroke the mythic behind you—Caribbean gothic style—catch you walking dead man hours dey so with them white handle razor. And Bo's girth retained that seed and his throat the melodious lilt of barrackyard lingo. And when Bo came to rassle was with high hat flippin' and a robber talk which induced cognitive dissonance. He manipulated deft verbs and lingual tourniquets with ferocious grace. And with ease he would then crack conks split with a thick guava stick or blaze fools strict with a sawed off laser whip.

Bo smoked zutz of dank bearded weed wrapped in brown paper—guma guma—till tongue-tied. Wire kept his boots tight. Upstairs Houdini's, behind the jamette harem, fatback Bo Nuggy paced a small room well hid and lit by a bouquet of candles. Bo Nuggy sweats, wipes. A dark green grease that stains a rag reserved for washing arse and stands beside a window, shifting the curtain with thick ringed fingers. Across the bay, he sees the luminous reds of Joe Sam's engine hummin' comin'. Some junker fiends been waiting for the prime melocyte oil. Since Joe been gone they been hungry for crisp vials and now they start swell up the entrance to Houdini's; bulbous eyed and sunburnt, venal for a glimpse of Joe arriving, somersaulting in their skins.

"Leo look the Congo pump coming! Run crack Whisky, bus' Gin!"

"Joe know Abobo in 'e arse but he back broad, know to separate dey bone from dey marrow."

"Joe deals it proper Paco, he doh eat nice y'know. Is liver oil an' dasheen, whole cowfoot and butterbean he so swallow whole."

With a heaving hum the chrome Congo pump came sweeping down from the darkness. It hover rode the sleeping tide with antimatic suspension, hissing imploding air, sparks buzzin'round the beam core. And a few pale coons run down to the jetty when they hear the locomotion. Bo Nuggy grinned but his sphincter quivered as the Congo pump settled on the waterfront. And a sly bead of sweat slid down his neck and chilled him to the wire. If he looked hard enough he could see Joe Sam step down from the ship, knockin' wrists with waterfront bandits, grinning tears of coins. Bo Gut big, but he 'fraid to temper Joe. His back bend tight, he pray,

"JoJoJoe Sam coming, Good Lawd, have mercy-e on my black arse tonight!"

Elements: of the living eye are. Seldom dealt with.precision.
most ways sideways inverted. Or abstract. When there is separation
between act. and observation/action and cognition. Notating delays
the true trajectory of biological dust and signals instead to relay
decoys. These decoys or possibilities themselves become part of
the view to be captured and are so: essential to any understanding
of motion or cognitive dissonance. Essence (itself).is an abstract
object. It cannot be brought back from a dream.

8

Extending Out to Brightness

since foreday dawn we come down splashing the dust of nefarious stars! and while our gods sleep we steal their masks and exhale completely, blow gauge/ bathe in mud and dip in tar and warrior red, gargle hot rum and spit fire, pump biscuit tins slack with rhythm. clap clangin' hub caps and iron, knockin' rum bottle with spoon and crook sticks. we coming down! blowin' conch shell an' singing, anointing our bodies with liquid light like blue we blue, we red, we black. magenta. silver striped, satyr tailed—scars of white paint.

powder smoke billow from sailor mas, calabash green, wild
island gold. but some colours cannot be deciphered by the
bare hearing eye. and the sound: brass wrestles wounds
through asphalt, steelband jammin' like they bound to
make a body make a body leap arcs of abandon, take days
to come down. drums like cathedrals tumbling. hi-hats reel-
ing sparks like cutlass lashing de road—hot so hot even
thumb tacks moan.
but some sounds cannot be measured—
      . . . and a muscle in the air.

this floating island spun centre of the earth as an epicentre
of all things sensual. here we measure time by temperature.
distance by breath, prefer death by fire. revellers, we as
dense as wet gravel down henry, george and charlotte
street, all the way down to the jetty in a vast and surging
kaleidoscope of blazing fire mas.

≈

wire frames support rabelaisian disguises, meticulous
sequins and fetish figures of startling silver worn swinging
with the hip shake/my chest gone tight as a warm drum,
niggerman, make the snare pop! sweet socalypso man
chanting till him heart bust an' big big arse rolling 'pon
truck top. grind mama grind and shake the firmament—o
gorm—no man can brace when the tempo
                                            .drop
it what make moko jumbie come down from the st ann's
hills—ten leg long, look! a shithound hoppin' through a
bush of masquerade boots—'e tongue heng slack like the
red bandana roun' he neck and he sniff and lickin' snowcone syrup, lickin' rum spit dried crisp on the hot so hot
heels leave holes in bitumen and sweat salt collects in the
gutters to dissolve woe within the flux of blood and spum
and bile and funk piss grieving through muck and breast-
milk like kingfish liver oil.

immortelles are in bloom of electric orange in memorial
square. and on this festival road, every flag that slap my
face is a blessing for exile. then a chantwell come his come
from up duke street, strumming bones on a bamboo saxophone, leading a mud mas band and 10,000 watts of wild
island jazz on a mack truck back. down in the engine room
the bass man start pump an' the drummer knock claves

and the horns leggo bop and the whole band ketch a vaps
and start churn a revel rhythm/ congas run amok like foot-
steps of runaway slaves.
well saturnalian ointment begin to bead like salt butter
saliva—and a river of arms rise up when the singer chants.
his voice moves like mad-bull kite in dry season. much like
syrup dripping from a guava tree, such like thick black love
dripping like the blood of gabriel into an old mans' eye as
he reclines—hung over the door for good luck but blinds
him cold
when it
      drop.
and the brass band begin to push past the park for the big
yard stage.
but some of us are shaking and some of us are waiting
for the fruit to fall.

~

sleeping in double-deck hotel bed reminds me of weekends spent with my mother in her matchbox apartment up ramkissoon trace and the hot light that slid through the bedroom louvres when the sun came down hard on the hill. saturday morning, her ovaltine enamel blowing steam through both rooms. and the pure face of my brother in technicolour gabardine and cowboy embroidery. my stiff blue shirtjack and brown leatherette boots. and our mother behind us with her fists on her hips, her big leg in red, the stern grin in them drag brother beads, her bosom strong with both breasts then and her soulcage sturdy on strap up sandal heels.

jourvert morning mud mas—she love that. would come home tight and multicoloured. monday she would play real rebel mas—washanti, wild indian, jab molassie. but every carnival tuesday she would take us downtown to memorial square to watch the bands parade. she'd lay a plastic tablecloth under an almond tree and bring out kool-aid, fried chicken, stew peas and macaroni pie from her basket . . . then sudden so a bottle would crash—a rage would rise— and just outside the national museum on frederick street —the band will slack—masquerader go scatter—some man head bust—vendor stall fall—limbo leg go wobble—moko jumbie jump down, another get cutlass clap and run. but

is so blood does come down sometime and just sweeten the
revel lil'more.
leave some of us shaking and some of us waiting
for the fruit to fall.

9

THE GENETIC MEMORY OF ANCIENT ÏERÈ

Realtime Trajectory of Explicit Love

From where they lay on the wooden floor they could hear the rippling tones of rubber on steel coming from the panyard down below. See, this was Carnival Friday night and a steelband were busy invoking rhythms long thought lost on sawed-off tenors, double seconds and quadraphonic steel. Night-long perfecting the rugged polyphony that travels through the valley, caressing every track and squatters' shack and causing pitch-oil lamps to blink on the hillsides and pawpaw trees to quiver in the melody. Is a solid/steady breeze that carries the bitter scent of citrus, coconut oil and sugarcane brandy up from distilleries on the edge of the city and the tincture of fresh paint from the midnight robber's collection box.

~ and a muscle in the air ~

He mother did never like me. She say how I wild an' tell 'im watch we October woman. 'Bout how my mouth go put me in trouble, an' how I does prance an' shake my arse like a Jezebel. But he come smooth like a saga boy, talking sweetness—know to make me laugh, eh heh? When I ketch myself is pregnant I pregnant oui. An' even still the woman use to watch me cut eye an' squeeze me like hinge as if she and she son was too good fo'me. But I come up strict strict, I didn't know slackness, my father name Mr Reginald Gonzales, he work tutty years in the St James infirmary an' was never late once, never miss a day. Then he use to come home an' grind tapia till mornin'. A man like he coulda never raise no jamette!

He feels the parabolic curve of her thighs against his, he cartographs her skin, the hot flesh of her inner thigh. His palms caress the upper cusp of her sun kissed hips. She surveys the scope of his back and plays scales on the flute of his spine. Her grip is stronger than he imagined but her breath is the tender texture of his dream, and her lips are creole chocolate. Between her breasts he finds talcum powder. And salt. Each motion of flesh on flesh occurs in a perpetual now, within the moisture of their embrace. And the water they make seeps through the floorboards to find ravines and runs through the anxious streets, filling the valley. Drowning all sound for a moment.

Gemma? Boy, I remember the firstime I see she. She was young, 'bout 17. An' I see this s-w-e-e-t brown skin gyul crossing Bagatelle Road and my heart jump dudup dudup. She as wearing a lil' green crimplene dress that ride up higher at the back when she step; was so the bumbum did fat! Well boy soon's I see she was like my blood ge'hot one time. Ah see she take the hill and jus' throwin' waist, throwin' waist. Ah say t'myself: nex' time, a mus' rap to she. Well boy one day I jus'come from wuk down south, rain like peas, an' I going through the Croisee. When I look so I see Ms Lady in a blue hot pants suit, stand up under Ackbarali's sheltering rain. Well thank god that day, I did have my umbrella.

He wears a black stove-mouth suit, white shirt, black tie, white gloved hands and grins beneath his centre-part. Her arm, in his elbow's grace, a gap in her smile. Her hair brushed and pinned behind a silver tiara. Angular sketch of her bridal gown. Anthuriums and lilies in her bouquet. Behind them are hibiscus branches and the leaning road, peripheries of dust. Her lace veil fades to the right of the frame but her blood was so close to her skin then. She would rail! Like that night by Jogie Road sawmill when she shred his shirt and ripped his cheek.

I remember that night. I almost kill 'im. Ah scratch way 'e neck from he navel, ah bite up he chest. But a-a, I tell Mr Man I want my child and he start to guff up. Ah bite till he put 'im down. Between he and he mother in my arse I get damn vex, I did fed up. So I take my child same night, an' walk up Ramkissoon Trace an' gone back by my

*father. But my blood did sweet for the nigger man still . . . and he
uses to come an' go. Next thing y'know is big my
belly big again. And my father say— "But wait, yuh mad!? You cyar
mind two manchild in my house!"*

　　　　So one had was

　　　　　　　　to go

10

On Kunu Land

That's the law around here, y'gotta wear your sunglasses: Starchild

Miss Selma knew. Knew when she came to Kunu Supia, first thing, was to tie her coal pot foot to her bedpost. 'cause she could cook them old sweet hand Sunday food good. Selma cook curry river crab and granny cow-tongue dumpling, hog head souse with roast breadfruit, white yam an' manicou. Guava jam and 'guana stew, grouper leg, 'gouti, Lappe an' Quenk.

Roast scorpion is antidote against its sting. Carambola has no shell. *Calling or in flesh . . .*
with a slice of avocado on the side.

56

Most time you could smell Selma brown sugar chicken from way 'cross the bauxite farm. Make people say,

"Weee Pa! Selma like she now throw some chicken in a dutch pot an' me doh mind suck the oil from the bone, ah eating skin an' all."

And when the sun shift Miss Selma would throw a thanksgiving. And have a holy man drill a loaf of bread with appointed finger. Pour olive oil. She lay a table of sweet meat and strange fruit. But was her black cake that make Kunu people ketch genetic backslap. Asking—

"Did I walk through the desert to get here?"

But Miss Selma would never teach nor tell, the press roll that kept her pepperpot hot or the mysterious ingredients she deciphered from extinct texts or else heretics would negotiate her pot for the secrets it held.

She died while tracking Shadon Beni bush in the savannahs, her secrets kept.

∼

Alfred Mac was a shy, bionic tailor, a black chinee afraid of even his own shadow. He moved through Toucan bay like a sand snake in a chiffon suit, carrying a briefcase packed with formulas for authentic zoot suits with high waist gabardine gunmouth slacks that fell just right over hi-top sneakers. Also beige flannel bellbottoms of the type ol'time grandfathers adultered in, low crotched khaki and double breasted shirt jacks. But when he bust price make Kunu people moan.

Alfred Mac owned a souvenir shop in the market square where he sold bogus etched gourds and leatherware, drag brother sandals and bamboo saxophones, grimy copper bracelets salvaged from a flood and other extinct para-parhanelium. He hung his red jute jumpsuits and bespoke waistcoats from the ceiling. Vipers robbed his shop several times, locked his neck to loot his stock but Mac boil rugged one day an' bust 'way they carapace with a tamarind cane.

And when Mac died all they found were forty-eight jazz cigarettes and a batimamselle nest in his navel. It was only when they pull for the posie he kept underbed that they discovered the private stash he'd amassed there in that secret underlung.

And for that they buried Alfred Mac face down in the hard sand of the Kilgode Delta.

Objects recovered from the Secret Underlung of Manfred Ayoung aka "Alfred Mac"

7 strands of hair from a sphinx's goatee, a facsimile of Michael X's bio manuscript, 1 sequin studded ladies purse, super-8 footage of Swamp Dogg and Solomon Burke by the sea, a substantial amount of peritoneal dialysis swill, 1 crocus sack of sundried chicken wings, 28 gallons of illegal rice, surrealist butter, ram goat liver oil my grandfather used to cut his toenails with shears like these sawed off cutlass blades, solid state dream recording equipment, Cornbread, Earl and Me with a white handle razor, 2 bamboo flasks of tripe and split-pea soup; one, a chrome plated grandmother's leg, snakeskin voodoo masks, jake

quantities of Nigerian cheese, bullet-proof pyjamas, jawgrind pornography, Dr Eustace Willie's Oxford shaving razor, smoke screen camouflage for shoplifters, 85 live crabs in a powdermilk pan, loose steatopygic bumflesh in jars, black hash in bogus afros back from Timbuktu pairs of sharkskin brogues with razor bladed heels, 1 wasp-waist liberation jumpsuit, copious amounts of old nigga spirituals preserved in paraffin, 2 pairs fisherman visors that clip on at the temple bone, 1 holy blue enamel pan cup, 1 gun make out a wood, 1 bull cock whipping blade soaked in catpiss an' pepper, 1 grinnin' afronautic helmet fulla red eye jumbie beads, 1 pair of unworn grey leatherette shoes, limbo stick hop like Legba goodfoot—1 toenail, bois bande seed, 2 blue vials of smelling salts (Ammonium Carbonate), 1 cold dose of Senna Pod tea, bikini no name, dead people jaw plate, 1 moist leather-bound Sankey Hymnbook, Swamp Dogg—Total Destruction—near mint condition, Freddy Fender, Jim Reeves for Sunday, Skeeter Davis, Betty Wright, O.V. Wright but

> Donny
> Hathaway

11

Whisky Lip Papa

my father hunts in these hills. for bush meat. for iguanas
and morocoys in sleeping streams. for agouti, armadillo
and quenk. he stalks the overgrowth with a thick silver
torch that stuns its prey sudden and a lance cut from green
bamboo and tipt with an old cutlass nib. he opens his
fridge; stale pig-foot souse and golden ray margarine, shark
sliced in garlic and lime and rum bottles of rain. but then
he takes a stiff bag from the freezer and says,

"manicou yu want? *steups*, well boy is every night i could
eat manicou if i want. sometimes is five and six i come back
wid from the bush. it have plenty manicou up in the bush

man, real meat . . . sometimes i flash one in a tree an' see it
have young, i does leave it."

D. marsupialis insularis (Didelphyidae)

the animal has been deeply gouged. its body scorched,
shorn of fur and disembowelled. poisonous mysts have
been removed from behind its ears. its frozen snarl is
clenched in a grimace like grains of rice on the wooden
mask of nommo, perforated at the gills.

out on the hillside the ground is still warm. from here see
the city lit and beyond; beads of light stitching sea to sky.
my father divides the manicou into joint, rib and splinter.
he scrapes burnt bristles from the tail. he splits the skull
and washes the pink flesh with lime, fresh thyme and
congo pepper. he builds a three stone fire and oils his iron
pot to fry onion, green garlic and geera. then pausing to
light his cigarette he says,
"stew?, stew is fo' dem yard fowl, way them hard so, to cook
for long, boil down. but manicou? manicou make for curry

boy, with coconut milk, thick sauce, uuhmmm," he licks his fingers, "uunmmm."

my father cracks the white oak seal and tips the first splash for those too dead to drink. and while we sip its vapour, he tells me about his father, lionel. a tailor by day, mattress maker by night, he was six foot six big with a hop an' drop walk, upright in the jaw bone braced his handsome blackness, with his gold teeth grin and his stingy brim trilby tilt, and his charm as slick as brown-eyed molasses. he bump down belmont valley road draped crisp in stove mouth slacks or pleated with the fat knees and peg top in doeskin, shirt tuck in. he bump through corbeau town in two tone brogues and flashing handmade rings on eight fingers. and the pimps, saga boys and jacket men would call out when he strolled,

"lio, o lio! run sometin' nah?" 'cause lio was a duke around. but under the floorboards of east dry river he drank coarse and copious amounts of hot puncheon rum while he stripped coco fibre for wire. he'd grind his gum till dawn as he worked a mattress, listening to a radio he hung from a nail. then to rise in the afternoon to twist seams, to line lapels and to suck more gin and wild indian wine while stitching suits for country christenings.

my father says, "i was working on a school down siparia, an' when i reach home—braps! jus so—i hear, my father dead.

an' i bawl—'no lio!, oh lionel!' 'cause that was my father name."

but time he dead he couldn't even drink water, all from he throat here down so was raw and busupbusup like he liver did grind way long time and he never tell nobody, the man was sick and still sharin' licks. but 'lionel' . . . that was my father name."

12

Aranguez

By early September, by the time she brought her first daughter to the gate, newborn and wrapped in white cotton powder, the revolution was dead. And new calypsos were already being written about that March, when the East Dry River broke and tumbled into the city, smashing shop windows, throwing bottles at the police—running; some with one shoe dragging, dodging baton and hard cuff, pulling crocus sacks of patent leather handbags, ham and shoe dye, Berec batteries, and English toffee up the hill with teargas in their eyes.

The revolution died because the masses—although

bitter—wanted simple things like running water, tele-
phones, indoor toilets, some wanted Sealy posturepedic
mattresses and Redifusion discograms. They wanted relief
. . . release. But reform is never revolution see.

"Rever what!?
Dat sound like war to me,
revolution?
Dem black power boys could talk dat talk 'bout
Neo-colonial, Post-colonial, Afro-Saxon, Pan-African.
But in John-John shantytown rat still killing man,
saltfish expensive, dollars scarce like hen teeth,
Banga seed falling from the sky!
an'all we have down here is big stone
and sawed-off cutlass.
Dem black power boys only making fist an'
rappin' 'bout BLOOD.
But when bullet start to pelt
an' teargas spray, they scatter—dashiki speed out like
      stingray,
jump in jeep and head for
the university.
That is why they band they head with hair.
So when de mark bust,
bullet go bounce
            right off—
                  they afro."

In those days the jamette was not allowed in the yard.
Was for what they called: her jezebel ways—a—a! And that

same strong, ghetto pepper mouth would hold no water to
cuss 'n shout—she'd shake the wire fence, she'd rackle on
the gate.
And was all them suffer she take what give she breast
cancer

From twilight under the orange tree she'd plead and
moan until even the dogs stopped barking. The old woman
peeped through her curtains as fireflies lit the savannah.
She remained silent and safe, only a radio possessed sound
in her kitchen.
"This is radio 610, time is now 7.49 and this is the Jackson 5."
And leaving the jamette to the stars would find her
grinding salt from her eyeballs. . . .
"Oh baby I was blind to let you go."
But that morning my mother brought my sister to meet
me, my grandmother let me and I ran to the gate, I was
three . And I can still see the gap between my mother's
teeth when she said,
"Is yuh sister y'know, y'want to touch she? Touch she
nah, doh frighten, is yuh sister . . ."

And I put my hand through the gate and held her

tiny

fingers

13

Ace Cannon

Joe Sam arrives at Houdini's with immaculate precision, stepping tough 'cross the floor as slick as vampire brows. Six foot six of rigorous black muscle in an oxblood ceramic polyester suit cut sharp with grey paramilitary pimpstripe; secret pockets packed with bootleg melanin, with glory rolls of edible money concealed in his bullet-proof waistcoat.

And how he strides: soulful, slappin' palms with the rugged grace of a southern Ethiopian cowboy. With battle scars on both cheeks and a leg long three-canal cutlass tucked in his waist with just the pelmet showing. Known

felons scamper hid in door hinge shaft. All wine stop wine.
And Mokotux Charlie come caliping down from his jamette
harem to grin like horse teeth and embrace the great man,
    "Ai Joe, when you reach? When you goin' back?"
'Cause Mokotux knew there was terror stalking Joe wherever he may go like Dravidian Indian suicide for phos-
phono.
    "Eh Joe? But you ban from here? You just hop go be
fight, ah beg yuh doh wruck up this place tonight. You
mark to dead—o gorm, Abobo in yuh arsss!"
Joe just grins. He must've been aware of motives installed
in these and other devious assassins for his demise, but as
he moves through the crowd his jaw is locked rigid and
reveals no fear. He steps to the bar,
    "Scotch and dry lime, plenty ice."
And the barman run Joe glass, as whispers teased in the
shadows. A shuffle of boot/gym boots of cautious killers
plotting to bust, and women straining their jewelled necks
for a glimpse of Joe's handsome face, with his head held
high and dignified, defiant with his loose cornered smile.
    Madame Sweetbum peeps over the banister to grip sight
of Joe as he leans on the bar with his grin stitched back.
And with her beads hung between her breast and head-
phones around the lucid blue silhouette of her afro, she
sees Joe Sam in flesh and the grim liquor she sips runs the
wrong throat when she ketch Joe eye—choke? She almost

tumble—into a pail of water—like a dream she had.

Sweetbum blood did take Joe Sam. Since that night she see Joe bat a man from Morne Poui Bay with a Bong tree branch an laugh. See him dance Kalinda in the grassland and she was hypnotised by his brown sugar charm and the hummin' bone he stroked. The way he leapt around the gayelle like a walking snake, the way he crooned deep soul when he itched to bone.

Madame Sweetbum see Joe Sam pass and her heart beat-up like frizzle fowl neck get cut and she reel an' turn a roll, start spin Ace Cannon on her gramophone. When Joe hear the honky tenor man blow—was the son of a preacher man—a gland raise and he begin to bob head, feel sweet an' leggo a bop from hip to elbow—make Kunu people go "OooOoo!" And giddy hop-hop hooray to see Joe dingolay.

∼

In the basement blues dance, more mellow the texture. Southern fried soul and incense burning like a leg and lumber room. Swamp Dogg, Solomon Burke, soft lights and dope smoke, lovers kept the walls erect. Citrus pungent drunks lay sprung on silk cotton sofas cradling demijohns of mountain dew while some puffed genk and rapped in the stairwell, making cuss words hop n'dance in eclectic

light. In a corner, pious old Ïerèans with grey long beards
an' beads of insect bone sucked bongfulls of black Tobago
gungeon and shuffled decks with feeling, sat round
plywood tables slapping harsh cards down—
"High low jack game!'"
"Who draw jack a dimes?"
"Bucky you plait dis pack?"
"Ace is mine!"
"Slam yuh spades Mr Buller, come ... Yes Poopa!"

Meanwhile back-a-yard side a corridor kitchen, one
mako iron pot of smoked Manicou soup sat bubbling nice
on a pitch pine fire. An old ragged dread with prosthetic
wrists bends prodding lumps of pumpkin, yamatuta, cow
tongue dumpling and green banana with a wooden spoon,
and the scent of lime, wild thyme and shadon beni rises
from the broth oozing a musky sweetness round the
crowded room. Something in the aroma invokes cravings
long thought lost in a young man with a pointed beard and
he comes nearer, to peep the pot.
"Whayahadey Rasta, some kina swrimp ting?"
And the old wooden dread turns with one eye dead, one
green and bulbous glowing to speak with a voice strained
in hyperproof babash,
" No I-ah, dat is de Manicou brain."
"Mani who?"

"Mani-cou I-ah."

"What! But dread I never know you could get jungle rat here. So much time I try bring back bushmeat from dream —but Manicou, yes, give I the tail Rasta."

When the young man taste the sweet meat so, and suck the bone and chew finger, make him go sit in corner write poem.*

Joe Sam take centre on the upstairs dancefloor. He cleared his throat and the din then drop, say,

"Well if you pale cool brown skin high yellow drum skin fresh water coffee tan backra beige Creole gold red or chocolate buttermilk better fortify your marrow or sun go bite you. This will even eradicate marasmus and cancer of the lymph, cure tobo foot malkadi, gout and backwash psychosis, put it in your hair—watch that covenant grow like mangrove sugarcane—halo glow round your conk and cosmic eye, as sure as pyramids were designed to be seen from the sky. An' if in four days that nose don't snap back wide, mammy must've rubbed it straight with coconut oil when you were a child, but never mind, just to squeeze a vial a' this bootlegged pineal oil should slap that nappy greng-greng wide open! Like slavery never was. This 'ere some uncut grease from the black gorgon bone/extracted by fibre optic syringes, resistant to alkali and ascorbic acid, government issue so bogus synthetic—giving nigger liver colic."

And soon quick his slim glass vials of nigum vitae had pale folks and tourists in a line. But steely eyes were scoping Joe Sam's throat, a wink in the awning sleek like kung fu slippers and the tense begin to bubble like somn gon burst, make Mokotux moan,

"Joe a beg yuh doh run no more dem vials here—place hot—doh blood—o gorm, do not upset."

Joe Sam just laugh. He must've known there were henchmen and hired hit men waiting downstairs to bust his craw, but as he strode towards the spiral stairway the crowd lie side like sugarcane, 'cause he strides so slick and wicked, so dapper majestic. It is obvious he carries mysts and secrets in his underarm socket.

*Humbone

You slept in spitty chambers, on a bed of salt in the market.
You said your skin was too tight, but even tight
can't hold you.

I saw you catch that star and put it in your mouth
and then wipe your lips on the table cloth.
And since then my eyes be ever longing
for the pure memory of a face
that won't contain you
no more.

We lit a fire in the sky and the moon saw who, sent
          splinters flit
over bridges, rivers and contours. Know that the blues
is a hummin' bone
a hummin' bone,
a blues protracted.

butter/kiss

I imagined rumours and scars but the apex was deeper still

I saw you blush with rage, trip past in your fever
with dry ice blowing
from your grim mouth. And your eyes
clearly seeing sound
but even sound
could not
con/tain you
no more.

14

Caura

macaripe

this wind is a blanket let blown from a storm
~ fireflies ~
startle dogs in the yard, make them call to each other
across the hiss patter of rain that must circulate to
feed the entire island.

there are men on the ragged pier. fishing and cooking the
fish they catch. brine smoke billows up from their coalpot's
grill and upwards to the burning hills where bush fires
have left the vegetation charred, a dirty brown. but the sea
is gentle here. and deeper where the water expels the light;
from aqua green to opaque, steep.

a swami seems to meditate in the splash of the surf. he lies supplicated on the wet sand and wrings his beard—undulating wave of white muslin—lets his body roll with the late morning tide.

the skeleton of a sea almond tree extends a callused limb as if to touch the ocean . . .

her feet step like light across hot sand, jewels on her toes

tairico

a man comes down from the rugged hills above tairico bay.
he hop down a jagged ridge, shifting bush with a cutlass
and carrying a vine of river crabs. he wears a stained white
vest, dirty jeans and muddy rubber slippers, carries his
young son on his elbow.
"twenty dollars for the whole nine redman, these now-now
ketch."

he lifts the bundle: each purple crab back\s shine is tangled
tight within the other, their hairy limbs and porcelain
claws are shut with vine. their eyes are beads that swing
and shut. mud clogs their mouths. while i pay him, a dry
coconut falls to the sand like a fist to a drum and the
hunter cleaves it quick with his blade and make we all take
a sip.
"see redman," he says, "even coconut for yuh curry."

and early this morning while she slept i drove down near
the city. came back in the full bright to wake her with an
iced birthday cake, little candles and champagne. but what
she wanted most she said, was to go to the sea again, today.

Caura

at caura river pounding rachette pods with a flat stone on
the river bank, between sparkling stones there are husks of
dried bamboo — razor blades and clay deya lamps. hindi
hair tangles moss at the waters edge. caura river runs with
the sunlight licking every ripple as it slithers brisk past
through so many shades of green. river hair. luminous fish
and moss weed.

to get here we drove upward miles past the chest hospital,
round and along mountains, through tonka bean village,
where panyols still ride humber cycles in muddy water-
boots through the ancient cocoa bush. from here we see the
islands true trajectory
              —extending out to
                 brightness

old caura sprung from ïerèan settlements. lokono indian
and black chinee came from mainland maracaibo. nepoio
and yao. then spanish come up from madamas bay through
santa cruz valley. and up to when cipriani plane crash,
conqueros still grew rich cocoa and coffee. and midwives
fed mandrakes white rice in ripe gullies.

but the village has long been reclaimed by the jungle. all

that remains are beads of steeple from a church; seeds of glass buried deep and overrun by thorns. and the bone dry tibias of runaway slaves.

but the river remains.

the same river that always led to this mythic place; this island's eden. once the gleam in the golden eye|age of cocoa.

and here the wreck of the derelict dam that never churned water is set back left of the riverside. its high gaping windows, red brick burnt, vines chew its hollow gut like graffiti.

manzanilla

out through this day here come another one.
she is up at 7.30. pale light, new eyes for new morning.
i saw this ::

a sloping road.
and driving down
with the sea on our left and the wind itself so bright.
we saw it clearly, it left a flash from the sunlight visible.

we drive through miles and more of lush island country-
side, along the rugged east coast, through citrus fields and
hog farms, through mountain towns and settlements of
windswept shacks. and then we see the flags planted along
the beach/ half a mile of flags and their clandestine shadows, like stanzas in place for baptismal processes. blood
red as such for a sacrifice. yellow for spirituality, resurrec-
tion brown slapping the salty gust. and then imagine a
forest of coconut trees with a hard black road shot straight
between and the sea brewing up on the left. and a vast and
barren expanse of sand, until the island seems to fade into
spray and white light.

the coast may break for rocks and reefs but the bay flows
from horizon to horizon. the sea pulls the sand open then

shut, reveals the stems of seagulls polished to pearl by
atlantic dust. blue water. coconut husks and seashells, drift
dried crisp in salt, brittle skulls of molluscs that crush to
powder underfoot, luminescent jellyfish veils. seablast
shivers the trees—a gust in the ear—and the sun . . .
the bay is as wide as memory

and we are alone here. in this sacred place.

15

Voyage to the Bottom of the Sea

The cosmic egg has fallen into the sea.
    The moon is as large as a large plate
    carrying a bundle of sticks.
    The sun rises from the sea,
        crick
            crack!

.it was about,
Bio/genetic dust. The texture of memory. Skin reveals a living history of the body. It is possible to see and touch these genetic memories. Milligan Benji, five foot nine and bone, standing on a hill overlooking the luminous city, barebacked with a Gilpin cutlass between elbows, sweat

oozing from his solar capital like government juice. Yawns/in the midday sun.

He was my age then and wore beige bell-bottoms over ten-eye high suede desert boots, overstepping streets and tree-lined boulevards in search of the carnival. But there are no masquerades on the avenues, no brass bands, no bamboo knocking—no wrist, no rubber, no steel, an absence of colour; the city seems ghostly bare. So he asks the dust,

"Where is the Carnival?"

And the dust replies:

"Many things begin
        and end in the sea."

*Me I half man/half nile crocodile. a'bad like dreadlock seahorse,
come up from the bottom of the sea, possessor of liquid textology!*

*Well I was once an upright walking man, till that day rain fall so
        hard
that it filled the valleys. Some fools try run an' hide up tree, but they
        drown*

*when the water rise. 'cause when the sea come up—it swallow the
        entire island.
Well, me and my family, we took a plywood raft to the open seas.*

*And for eight nights and days we survive on nothing but plankton
        and seaweed
till one by one me see dem drop. My daddy was the last
        to go.*

Then was that day a black rain fall bucket a drop and rivers rose over mountains. The storm sent shacks tumbling, the sky dim lit like a dream. Many skulls were bust just by the weight of raindrops. It rained all night till morning meet the sea capsize, 'cause in those days there was no moon.

Milligan ran to the high cliffs on the coast and found that many had already swum east from there. They left burning heaps of bed linen, dried fish and chamber pots of mud and manjak bitumen. And the bones of those the spirits refused flight.

Milligan saw the water coming over the hill behind him, flinging wood and beast like sorrow self. And seeing this broke him bare. The suffer the love, the suffer the love bore thick tears in his eyes. But you see my Milligan was a black heart man. He unlaced his boots, he removed his sterling silvers. And he bent his head in meditation at that steep brim between the gulf and the sea swept hills. He had saved many lungs of breath by then, in a sack hid under his armpit for mercy. And so, he just up and leapt into the sea below.

Now when I jump from that raft was sea snake an' catfish that guide me
to Olokun kingdom neat the bottom of the sea. And I see

my people swim free,

who were bound for slave terror but dove over like me, to escape

*by suicide—but did not die—they came here and were fed and
    healed.*
and now dey 'fraid to swim back
                    to Africa.

∾

When he really begin to swim so, he swim with slink
and mountain chicken, he swim with zangie eel and push-
ermen fleeing the island. He strong alone on the swirling
tides, four days clung to a macajuel snake that floated out
to die. Early on the fifth day he met a merman. And he
asked the merman,

    "Mister man, where my ïerè?"

And the merman replied,

    " ïerè dissolved in the flood like sugar in saliva, only
fragments remain."

    "And Africa?" Milligan asked.

And to this the merman calmly replied,

    "Many died"

Milligan swam with the merman to the outskirts of an
undersea kingdom. He had heard about this place from a
Baptist mythic, heard the pearl fishers' rum talk. But its
dimensions had long been underestimated by even
eminent cartographers. Milligan saw the black coral caves,

he saw intricate emblems stitched in bone. He saw hummingfish dart between his awe and personal temple. On the outskirts he could see the volcano plantation, spewing magma and pumice flame from the seabed. And he saw that when the molten stone dried, crests and valleys were formed and within these were crystalline segueways and subaquatic chambers where the niggerfish lived.

Milligan asked the merman, and the merman said, "Many things begin and end with the sea—indeed—the earth is hollow, not solid as was thought."

And such as these were the words that kept Milligan in Olukun's kingdom, till soon he would not notice water.

And it was

y   e   a   r   s

before we saw him again. Landslide scars. He sent no letters.

My skin become sealed with rugged rubber, my lung become tough with brine, my tongue become dank with word

: spitting: Obeah mantras, seducing spirit travellers. a'leave them hissing with lust
when a' bust they soulcage open like slavery never was / But if slavery never was,

Backra Johnny woulda still say,
*   "Well, if God made them black,*
*   it must mean something."*

We sang for Milligan across the ocean, we sent black-birds singing Flack and Hathaway. My grandmother said if we sang his name he would hear, would come running, would be there.

> *Iba Olokun fe mi lo're.*
> *Iba Olokun omo re wa se*
> *fun oyi o.*

. . . came back smelling of the sea.

16

Malkadi

Now when Joe Sam step down in the shebeen he crack
the whole vibe to a simmer, make people cease shift and
chat to gape at him roll, with his hat tip down and his boot
bumpin' 'neat steam pressed seams. Al Green begin to
moan—

"I can think of younger days . . . ."

And Mokotux come tumbling after, still weeping like
mosquito in Joe Sam ears, "Joe a' beg you doh run no vials
down here tonight—good lawd—go be fight—drum skin
bust!"

Joe turn and say, "I am Joe Sambucus Nigra, whom shall
I fear?"

Till soon some commotion start mumble an' hiss shooshoo in the shadows.

"Joe Sam ha'belly oui, come back here like he lookin' fo' dead"

"Mako doh watch Joe slight y'know, Joe deals in black/secret technology. Obeah, Shango or obi seed—is only spirit lash could hurt he so."

Now the basement was always Joe's domain. Here he often dealt in genetic contraband and got gutty with ïerèan vipers. Here he could rap plain like gazette paper in the long lost lilt of that old floating island. These rooms are dank with fisherman's musk and the grease of black folk tumour water. Swill dribbles from lurid wounds in secret rooms upstairs, burnt brown sugar and sweat rice settles in the ravine. But many nights Joe did knock back booze here and grin an' sop up souse water, flinging dice till dawn. Many times he dealt bitter justice in the maze of silent rooms beneath the dancefloor. Like once Manuel Gogo, a foul thief from Tobago did testify,

"If Joe Sam skin thick, a go throw fire in e'mudacont! Is a long time now I waitin' to gnash 'im"

Not so. Joe leggo a lion in his arse one night they clasht in the passway. Joe corner Gogo in an alcove and broke his floating ribs with a roti skin.

~

Some black hand pass a stick of red beard collie Sambucus way. The toke took Joe deep in a deep funk damp with the essence of danger. Assassin chair shuffling space to seize an instance to pounce. But Joe Sam busy shifting bootleg melanin for siderite stone till all the vials done and leave cripple crying in the line behind. Joe grins a wide arc as he takes his stand on a powdermilk pan and he pulls two tubes of his strictest line from an inside pocket and lays them to light. And a dozen more soft brown hungerers push to peep round his halo and start to hiss and plead. The mere sight of the serum causing some to salivate and somersault in their sufferin' skins—all skin teeth eh grin— but still they quick to shell out cash and coloroid stone for oil, balm or any pill to temper epidermis to the Supian firesky.

But then a blade flash from behind the organ and some-body shout— "Focker, you go dead tonight!"
And everybody mouth
          drop
          belly
          open.
But Joe had was to laugh.
And the bellow sprout :

"Yeah you laugh kee kee kee, a go show you
how r e a l nigger be!"
(Death spit a glint in the din. Red eye wide behind a bottle
of fortified bourbon)
And Joe turn beast for that, say,
"Who dare belittle my integrity?"
An' he step back spread, steady nostril flare, in one swift/he
unhinged his zoot jacket, revealing a wire-bound cutlass
handle hung from his waist. De blade old but it cutting
still, the rim grinning and snarling same time like when
rain fall and sun shine same time two Abobo man bust
through the crowd and start jump an' caray like crab. One
take left he had fire in a bottle/one take right with a scimi-
tar blade, one up in the rafters he name Manuel Gogo—he
black like ten crapaud in a pan, with a sniper's machete
and a bullpistle whip. He vex so vex he foaming at the eye,
and his neck is stitched with rage. His cuss spew so thick no
one could decipher, dig it, was like some dryfoot and
ancient badniggermantra that brought back more genetic
memory in the young man with the pointy beard stay writing poem by the latrine.[1]

Joe Sam strums his beard and then he calls to Mokotux
Charlie,

"Go tell Uncle Rampaul make three more cardboard
coffin, and see if Shoesman want these Abobo man hide to
build desert boots."

And an old mangled Rastaman start they griggling in a corner –"kee, kee kee." Abobo them guff-up and cuss with that, brandish long tongue cutlass. They crank an' jack horner Joe Sam against the bar top pine. Joe braced his stance and he fingered the clip on his blade, say say, throw salt.

"You think hero can die in the last reel?"

Then jus'so—BRADAX!—

hand pelt/bottle break/

table turn over.

Al green stutter then screech to a stop. I see Kunu people scamper manic in pleats and brogues, see woman hold they breasts and run. And more rush down from up to peep what gore. Joe Sam worked his blade within blinks/his cutlass sharp was laser bladed/it chop don't heal—and when it flashed it left one Abobo man pierced neat the gizzard and one back slice. Cancel all bets. But Manuel Gogo swung a blind and callous blade which cut Joe proper on the neck side—slit—but Joe's cutlass cuts cartilage/whipping hot steel across lung cage, to the body, round the waist. Manuel Gogo mince 'way, reaching for his back as if the wound did itch. A'fuss dem vex! One man spin miss kick fall down crack hip, next man fling sharkbone dagger, skin peel—get cut black on the comeback, swimming in bile neck deep. Manuel Gogo bawl like pig dem drag slit slaugh-

ter dem—he was already dead but did not know it and he
stagger up to grasp Joe Sam shirt an gargle,

"Ice in you ice Mr Joe, your blade like fire . . . from where
that forge?

And the old rastaman in the corner laughed so hard his
liver hurt, almost swallowed his tongue.

When Mokotux Charlie see blood spray and glass splat-
ter he run round the back go hide behind a plywood
commode. Was no easy scene. Just gristle an' blood flash on
the walls and reckless looting at the bar. And with a bevy of
henchmen still itching to bust, even Joe knew was time to
go. But when you look you see a haunting wound under his
armpit and blood dripping warm. He measures the wound

with a finger; was then he gulped the focus of suffering and had to steady himself on the stair rail. By the time he staggers from the basement, his jacket is crooked and damp with woe and his breath get snuff.

Up the dancefloor hot! Wet flesh and big leg swinging hip to that Spasm Band sound, Jah Stone on the bassline fully :
boomboom dada—b-boombadoom bama.
boomboom bama boombadoom daba
Make spirit bass rattle through the floorboards.
Madame Sweetbum, her nimble fingers on the stylus handle. And when the needle grips the brass round the centre pole, a tambourine ring and wow how the sax EXPLODE—it make Kunu people jump, sound them wail for they beat surrender. Joe Sam slip between beats but he fenky fenk with shaky feet. Come come pushing his sideways plead through the crowded room and out into the warm night with his blade hung down weak and his wound dripping oil. When Joe look behind he see more Abobo man keep coming up from hollow ground with shine eye blade. Run Joe run somehow sideways fastest. Poor Mokotux alone had to mop up the swill.

The blade that zugd Joe Sam was dipped in nanobyte salt that permeated his muscle and ate for the bone. When

Joe Sam get the burn, he groaned in his gut and cussed the unforeseen complexity and something like a sadness glazed his eyes. Leaning into the seawind he beat a crooked path along the quay, past the biscuit factory and the parallel market.

Joe Sam never complex to get cut. His slick sheen shut. But now his boot kicks dust as he seeks the solace of his Congo Pump. And was the first time Joe Sam, what once impervious to bone, at least make a bow to heaven an' moan from a mortal wound. Many beep hoot when they see Joe run but they still head hard to believe it. They come out peepin' in bullet-proof pyjamas.

Better run Joe

RUN!

1 . . . slow fade catastrophe
across miles and miles of secondhand teeth.
It could've been worse
but I didn'ven let 'im speak
befo' I bust 'im face with a Poui tree trunk
and see the lump ge'fat an' laugh—kee kee kee

. . . several witnesses did.
But some died owing evidence.
Some hid theirs in hills around the city
        —a dream of ruins—
and those who died in the ascent,
were left standing where they fell.

17

. . . Before Her Body Fell

santa cruz

i searched through dank wounds, dim lit and hollow tombs
to find her but only a resonance remains.
the sprinklings of her in steep pine crevices,
behind wardrobes for her laughter. her thumb
pressed light in glimpses.
i knew her sadness then and felt warm and alone in the old house
where sunlight spread butter bright on varnished cabinets, like
        water
from a viridian seascape. and the curtains swung in the living
        room.
la basse scent is stink till sweet, blowing up from shanty town,
blowing ghosts through each room.

97

. . . through cocoa country to my grandmother's grave in
the santa cruz valley and find it unmarked and overgrown
with weeds and churchyard mud. so i leave and call my
aunt from cantaro junction and she says,
"no, no, that not mammy grave. mammy grave have
concrete round it and a rayo tree plant in the center."

so i go back up, through the cathedral courtyard, where an
old man is washing a hearse and walk down into the
catholic bush again to find the grave on its east/west axis,
still next to the tomb i first thought was hers. just a rim of
unprimed masonry studded with stumps of all saints
candle root. but it is quiet here. quiet enough to hear a fleet
of cornbirds in flight or the whisper of wind between the
tombstones. peace in the valley.

the first time i saw her grave she was less than a week
buried. i sat silently at the earth of her bones as the midday
sun lit scents of cow dung and frangipani. she had always
said—"when i dead put plenty flowers on my grave."
and that day hers' was a mound of soft bouquets, wilted
heliconia and rotting white roses . . .

but the landscape has since changed; gravediggers have cut
paths through much of the bamboo that once shaded these
graves to plant more bones in the bush. the rayo stem set

centre has grown into a flag that tilts it's slender leaves in the loose breeze. deep purple leaves stained with dragons' blood. and many graves here share this configuration. tall rayo trees on the hillside coming down; from bone to root, ladders for spirits to cross.

tunapuna

she walks through dim lit rooms, utters
a phrase or two, her face
i merely glimpse. so profound, but in hindsight
i could not
define her. she suffers in a broken shack on a hill
that's bound to tumble
to ruins. mountains of ruins. she stands
in the courtyard of a derelict hotel. she stays
in a small room. ready with sacks of her possessions.
on the bed her wig and soft clothes, cold sweat
and cornmeal porridge. in a place where everything happens
    at once.

but o my mother's grave is so rugged and bare. there are no trees here in pasea village to filter the sun's flame, no flowers here except the dust of the moon. long grass curls and lizards shed skin on the sack of her bones. this is a parched field of withered sarcophaguses, skewed stones, burning bush and upturned earth.

machinery churns in the distance from a frying pan factory, pharmaceuticals, cola and plastics. the buzz of a school, wheels that hiss from the highway. or just a ram goat chewing weed to ring a bell round its neck. lovers rastlin' in a tree. crooked smoke from the coffin factory.

she helped me light candles that night when i was too weak
to eat and held me in the cut of her breast and stroked my
head and heavy shoulders. she fried bakes and boiled coffee
— carrot for wine, sugar for yeast. she lit a candle for sympa-
thy and said,

"the ol'lady dead boy, but at least you still have me"

but by then she wore a wig 'cause her hair was shorn and
under her fingernails she kept perhaps, dried molasses. and
her lips were red raw and her eyes hot with fear. till soon,
she too lay hard-to-dead and halfway between prayers and
vaseline, dialysis swill and spirits of menthol, rose scented
talc and strained pumpkin soup in ward 32, within a black
circle drawn around her life at port of spain general.
tighter. then than their/our hands could clasp in prayer.
until it broke her bulk of unconscious laughter. a catheter,
she said,

"they jook here with no anaesthesia"

she raised the sheets but i could not. look. or see her as she
was and not like we'd just met, in that pure time, on that
hot day. preferring to draw harmolodic portraits of her and
to hold her with arms i never knew could embrace her that
way. to suffer the love. to bring her grapes and cartons of
milk. money for membrane, brandy for cold toes. lavender
for pillowcase.

the ward smelled of burnt coffee and disinfectant. and how
the midday sun blazed the steel chimneys and blue smoke
out the morgue . . .

    i knew by the timbre of the phone i left ringing.
    she blinked, hard i heard
    but i looked away
    before her body fell.

18

Wallerfield

Dennis, that red nigger was strong. He did the bull work on the farm. He worked for food and shelter then he smiled. His mind reclined in madness but he smiled, big bush baby tears—wholesome and wide in the pouring sun. He grew freckles and trained chickens. His tongue was made of rubber but he smiled. Just doin' the bullwork on the farm. He chop the bamboo, he wash the yard, shovel cowshit, he bathe the heifer—dig that ditch!
Mrs Gray would say she found him by the river, but is run he did runway from the orphanage.

Doris Gray, her smiles were rare. But she grew amazing cakes those Sundays in Wallerfield. Home churned buttermilk, a slash of lime, living brown sugar. Fruit infused in eternal rum and aromatic tinctures. Head back and haughty she'd cock her ol' arse and open her oven and send the scent go roam across the pastures. But. Soon sick. Deep sugar, blood pressure, consumption, cystitis and lymphatic cancer. Her eyes fell out. Then both her legs were amputated. Wheelchair bound and disembowelled by disease, she hid twelve diamonds under her bed and stayed in her dim room while hard rain fell on the farm and I found her Jackson 5 45s in the trunk of a derelict radiogram. When she died, Gallstones came up the kitchen and said so. Sister Syl put a plaintive palm to her breast and said,

"O gorm Suggs, when she dead?"

"Six o'clock this morning she fall outa bed, when 'dolphus look—is dead de 'oman dead oui!'

Adolphus Gray had the slack thighs of an old man. Water filled his knees. He used to roll up to the cow pens with hands shut behind him. Grey haired, his gum grinning. In pressed chequered shorts and short sleeved nylon. He wash canister, he mix grain, he spin the salt lick—crack that whip! But soon sick. He caught a stroke. Death sharpened his toes. Then prostrate cancer wiped his gold teeth grin and skin gathered around his ankles like governor socks. With yaws on top of cocobay he gave up his gizzard for mercy and sold his cattle cheap. He gave Dennis a bill roll and let Dennis go and Dennis ran barefoot through the orange field. He gave Gallstones his silver plated cigar case and the beige Ford Falcon he kept tied in the shed and soon after that, shat himself inside out, and died.

But Gallstones, he was hard to dead. Shrunk-dried from diabetes, constipation and liver rot, he groaned for many seasons, dying slow for mercy, slow for mercy. His hernia hung stones in his passway as big as copranuts. All man dead and he sat crying in the toilet, pining woe in slow fade sufferation, as one by one his brothers fell, his good-good friend, but even then was ever quick to roar,

"You must take dis kiss-me-arse house for some open sepulchre! Go bring me de belt, a go bust you arse in two!"

He lock door, he bust leather—once he pull a gun, she had to hold him back and her tears became rain in my dream that night.

But some sweet Friday he may bring come: butter and egg or warm creole bread and fried chicken ice cream. And when he worked in the shed till morn was most times gentle. He worked meticulous wood. Crook sticks and crosses and chipwood commodes. He planed and grooved with silent strokes, never 'Pass tat chisel boy, pass tat plane.' Not even 'Brace this steady lemme shave this pine.' Just his gutty breath and the vapour of pitch pine burning in a milk pan to shade mosquito dust that drifted across the savannah.

They found him on the veranda.

19

Joe Sam Meets Bo Nuggy Uptown

Just past the geysers and the bullpen shuffle, round down the seaport; northwest tradewinds stir the sleeping sea, blow sand from the beach. Sulphur dust put sheen in lighthouse laser bulb beam. The figure stepped from the shadows wearing the wooden mask of nommo perforated at the gills and Joe Sam buck. The masked man stood wide and wore full midnight robber regalia: a big brim top hat and stiff-pressed cape, black satin tunic upright in the neck, black canvas slacks with luminous embroidery: four point stars, moons and intertwined spirals. His good gut adorned with sequins that flashed like shards of nebulous

lightning. And when he spoke this he did not stutter. Was
like a bass pan capsize on the barbergreen,

"Drop your stance Sambucus, yuh mark bust!
Know me, Bo Nuggy the midnight robber.
Clearly the most cantankerous and callous assassin your
    insipid gaze may glimpse while roaming contrary.
    Take heed when I kill, dust bury you where you lay.
My back well broad, my Gilpin cutlass lip sharp till it
    brittle.
Where I spit no man may plant corn.
Doh vex me grow two thunderstone horn.
Was tuttysix months I slept in the solemn chambers of my
    mama womb.
That when I was born a clap of thunder shook the moaning
    room,
bare hail of sun stone shower and whole stellar cities were
    left to ash
and planets plundered. I then set out immediately over
    deep oceans of space
to cause havoc wherever I as much as whisper
this robber talk.

I continued east, robbing and looting entire settlements
and spreading terror like a rake. I kill from priest to
    cardinal.
I jook from Duke to spook.
Some tests brave but I brutalise. I slit through their
    breastbones
with this cold bladed sabre.
They all fought bravely but I dismantled them completely

and set fire to their bones.
A crack dem conk capsize dem gizzard.
Me one an' I alone, a bad minded and evil midnight ripper,
ah bore dem up like strainer!

I was given systems and seals steeped in pits of sulphur by
     my father,
who taught me subliminally, the nomenclature
of midnight robber.
Till now I turn beast and conqueror
with eyes become seeds of serpents.
May death have mercy on you—my bulk will grow!
Better not buck and inveigle me to pounce,
better not plot, I suggest you drop that sack a' gene seed in
     your armpit.
If not I kick an' stab, same time split your skull asunder.
Chop when I cut bleed, e doh heal, I cut so deep,
it even leave mark in water."

Bo Nuggy bray then like mountain chicken, comin' to come now steppin' with his mottle cold blade. It narrow and long, it knotted in the middle like a dead Griot kneecap and the tip curled up and over back. And when he shook it left splinters of sparks in the hot dark. Joe gave a cold grin and stiffened the grip on his cutass blade hilt. But blood pulsed from his neck in spurts. Even so he growl,

"Come leh we punta Mr Nuggy—a go do fo' you!"
And he wiped the Abobo grease from his blade to a trouser leg and he start crab-step the midnight robber.

Joe Sam belly deep. He ruggedy steep, but weak. He never glimpse a glint of eyeball twitch behind Bo's beaded mask, till he taste the first blow peel a pulsating wound across his chest. The edge bit through his waistcoat, penetrating chrome. And he staggered back and put a palm to the gash and gasp,

"Is so?" In a voice not as deep as before, "Who send you?"

But another lash slit his hip. Between blinks he sees himself smelling his fingers, the same fingers bending wire mas for wild Indian tiaras, smoking dry ice, Mingus, through a chicken bone. And finally Joe give a groan to mercy. Bo Nuggy brace.

"Gimme de pouch Sambucus! If seeded would sprout . . ."

An he swung his blade again. But Joe spin quick this

time and the laser whip miss, he broke Bo's tibia with a roundhouse kick. And the full bulk of Bo Nuggy was shook fundamentally. And he bent to tend the torn bone with a selfless sigh. And when Joe Sam gashed him 'neat his navel deep, his gut bust, crack both knees when his big body drop —let sea cockroach and halibut fall out, and bawl :

"EGBE MI O!"

Like ten tarzan and tumble down in the sand.

Joe Sam scoped Bo Nuggy's craw and saw where it was vulnerable, came up behind and locked his fat neck with a phantoms grip/two fingers up Bo Nuggy nose hole and rips, unmasks him—wood from bone—skin from skull—hat from scalp. And underneath were circuitries and weaves of wire, blue wax and all kinda old iron an' ting. And something that smelled like pissfunk ammonium. Poor Bo just roll in the gully root and he body start to beat up

beat up

beat up . . .

Joe Sam severs a crooked path, his power fading, though the black electric night and the soft asphalt alleys. He drags himself through dregs of an abattoir. Sambucus suffer. While pitch oil stay burning in the all night Roti huts and bush wine sapping ol'man shin bone in the convalescent dome. He ran sideways fastest as if in dream speed. Some say he seen near the jetty but no one knew where. Some say concentration on the solar plexus had rendered him invisible. Some say he stash a bag of gene seed in a verge. Some see blood and >blink< to change the scene. Some say was seasnake take Joe where he dwivé and dive. Abobo ranger seek nightlong with fibrous infra. But by dawn the Congo pump was gone.

20

Crown of Thorns

they have desecrated the garden. replaced it with lawn
grass stolen from the savannah: arid and raw like a burnt
corpse's chest. wind hot with bitter to dust blowing like
scorn across the dirt this february's dry season. but this
field seemed wider then, when i used to hunt horned
beetles there or shake rose mango trees in the indian farm-
land. villas crack the landscape to the left where years ago
ignacio lopez lived in his slate roofed mansion; maided and
bulldog, barbwire guarded. and not one mule on the plain
or the blackbirds mammy would throw rice to over the wire
fence.

she tended and moulded her garden like a child brought up from stem. she kissed ferns and fed hummingbirds dry skin from her palms. and churned the soft earth for forty years 'neat the tropic of cancer. each morning, she would rise with the dawn and slip her toes through a ragged pair of the old man's brogues, her weight crushing the heels. she would pour cold urine at the root of her ceboletta tree and anoint the balisier spears. she bends to gossip with her marigold, she lingers at the chrysanthemum, to pinch a frond of aloe.

she knows herbs by their temperaments and can tell you every shrub and vine, every leaf, every pod and what what can cure. she'll say,
    "use roucou, use kush-kush grass, use zebafam, use shandilay. use spider lily or ground itch bush, try fever grass, shadon beni. use sweet broom or dité-péyi, boil bois cano with two obi seed, physic nut or gully root. use zigar bush, malomè, ti marie or jumbie bead, use shaddock root or nutmeg leaf. but dou-dou be careful with ceboletta please."

and when she died she left a stem of rayo in a glass and a hand of purple croton in the brass goblet beside her bed. a tattered mother's union bible, a red sankey hymn book, her hearing aid in its styrofoam box on the bedhead and a

teddy bear sent from london with a pink ribbon 'round its
neck. she must've known she had days to live when her
liver broke and her feet began to swell. she lay praying with
eyes crying stars, reciting intimate textologies.

rum in flask and corn in saucers, roses on the tablecloth.
and all the photo frames will be turned around.

but the old man adultered. he spent the same forty years
with his mistress too. a mistress bruce. a ol'hardback nigga-
woman grinnin' in a steam laundry behind the san juan
bridge. gaunty gaunt with them horn rim frame, cock-
mouth—her tongue was black—had to brace her wig when
he drove she and she children through bagatelle village in
his pumpengine jitney. He smoked a pipe then and strolled
in low crotch khaki, knocked gin and soda right, rum and
water tight by the time he bump home to cuss he wife.
    crick
      crack!
the floorboards creaked when he hung his hat—sparks
would reel when he wiped his brow!
    "look 'ere madam this food too damn hot!"
so she'd rush to blow steam from his cowheel soup or to fan
his pigtail stew. all those years she boiled ham and kneaded
dough and scrubbed his shirt collars till her fingers bled.
yet i never overheard him tell her. sweet things.

then that dim lit day, the sky was grey with the imminence of rain. she was burning garlic in a black iron pot and a fleet of scarlet ibises had just flown the savannah, when he staggered up the stairs with salt in his eyes.

"sugs, a had a blackout."

that was all he said. and for the next six months he spent in pyjamas, sipping fried milk in port of spain general. that christmas he ate no pork nor drank grog and was weak and both blind in most eyes by the time she took him east of the island to her kin for spiritual cleansing. and then for the next year, steamed his pumpkin right and fed him eggnog, prayer and split-pea porridge each morn until he could walk again, kick engine, beat snake, chop down them dead banana tree, lay drain, uproot cassava, skin iguana and sand teak for shepherd john crook stick. from then he knelt with her on sunday, sang and clapped hymns, saved her from falling when spirit-power shook. but he never stopped swing/

ing.

for the first of many mornings after she died, sylvia would return, to swim around the lower branches of the red poinsettia tree, to see the old man. and what did she see? she see he and madam bruce sat sipping cocoa tea in the foreday dawn. so sylvia become a hummingbird and fly back to heaven.

lef'im jus so.
let corbeau blow dust where he walk.
pour hot oil in his living eye.
he so go reach river jordan
and turn back.
bird go jook he jowl for vinegar seed, bush go bite.
jumbie go lock he neck with razor grass, rain go bus'e head
when it drop.
that night you hear a dog cry
is gone he done gone
breath get suck.

there are mountains to the north. but the earth is flat here.
there are no ferns there are no lilies here but the burnt
stump of a guava tree. there are no alocasias, amaryllis or
orchids. no more than just that old crown of thorns that
she smuggled under armpit from dense cocoa wood as a
sapling. it alone survived the drought that swept through
this yard and red flowers still sprout from its knotted stems.

sickness water mumbles. the old man sits in a wrought iron
chair with sick sunken eyes, wiping his rag with kanaga
water. his hollow chest heaves and he coughs, wrings his
dry hands are cracked like parched earth. groans so deep
with his brittle old carpenter bones he can hardly speak,
splashing spute on the cold terrazzo. above the door, the
angel saint gabriel wears a vest of roman amour and hacks
at the devil with his sword swung high, the devil on the

ground got his wings in a tangle.
struggle in his eye but still clappin' blades.

21

The 'doption

Remember when Sister Vero returned to San Rafael that Sunday, after the first time she went to earth? Was nine days she lay blindfolded in a room reserved for transcendence. With flags, bells and flowers, libations of oil and water, and diagrams in the dirt. That room was the ark of her covenant, her axis: the centerpost, her

: Jacob ladder

: Rod of Aaron

: Wood of Lebanon

And the cosmos inscribed in the rafters.

Blessed with madness and etheric sight, she'd

119

wandered crazed through catacombs and ruins of Akasic monasteries. And how she stomp side the pulpit that bright Sunday noon with candlewax gripping her crying hands. Was so engulfed by the holy spirit, she shook and almost capsize Zion fireside.

She wore the white gown and turban of the traveller. And carried a stem of Heliconia given to her by a merman. "Half man/half Nile crocodile," she said. "His eyes shone like sunbeams through smooth onyx bone."

And with a voice that whistled like slivers of dried flesh on a branch she began to relay multiple pages of transcendent jazz——the metaphysics of another world. Some return from the ground with a throne of grace and secret colours. Some come as pointers and provers, Sister Vero came back with instructions of purple and warrior blades. And that Sunday, we listened like hers was the last poem falling over an apocalypse. And was to see how Sister Vero swung her thickness as she testified, a–a. Well all the congregation could see the gifts she were given. And Leader Jimmy smiled. He could see her bosom was still wet from crossing River Jordan.

Was soon after that Jimmy seduce Vero. But poor Jim didn't know how Vero was fierce—Jim couldn't hold—when she back back, he roll. She shook him to the marrow! Broke his spring bed and blew his lungs full of grapes. And what Jim thought was just thick black love was really a serpent inside her.

And now Jimmy feel he alone must expel this demon. He whips his bell, so the congregation sing: low from the belly and clap from the hip. The hymn they swing become a rhythm for Jimmy to blow—make spirit power jump up in people chest real quick! Make them sing from the belly, and clap from the hip and sprinkle water to calm the dust they kick.

Leader Jimmy has a full head of hair but his woman is possessed by a speaking serpent that must be exorcised. And his neck veins strain from crying psalms round the centerpost. His robe holds four serious seals on his black satin stole :

Now when the drummer start work that holiness beat see the cane breeze break an shiver. And Vero struggle press against a plywood gurney. She overcome and fall. So the congregation gather round to peep, at Vero, rolling in the dirt, with her dress flung up, revealing the cusp of her black moan/spitting tongues with her eyes rolling round the back of her skull. And Jimmy too deep in spirit now to cover her up.

Was then Ma Mamin[1] bent to my ear, she said,

"Lil' boy move from there, let the ting come out an' pass."

But I kept looking, until I'm sure I saw the spirit print shift loose

> and rise <

¹ Ma Mamin's smiles were reserved for children. Her skin was the colour of sun washed avocado seed. Her full moon face shone bold and luminous. Ma Mamin: not bourne, she emerged from the rainforest whole. Rare herbs sprung from her navel.

In the room in which she kept her sacred artefacts and accessories, implicit fetishes hung in intimate places with beads, coloured stones and noxious oils, books of Eden's apocrypha. When Ma Mamin fixed the red band round her waist and rang her brass bell and walked the stretch of dirt

+++++++++ +++++++++

from her tapia bungalow to the church she'd built in the country bush, the pleats of her white gown would crack the wind, make blackbirds shiver and weep and cattle pull for home from the orange fields. It was Mamin who broke the old mans cataract. Who brought him back from darkness, who rinsed his liver with sweetbroom and honey, who soothe diabetes with shaddock and magnet root.

22

On Kunu Morn

Did I walk across the desert to get here . . .

Viridian sunlight illuminates Toucan Bay like silverfish net. This is the time of day when lice die in hair grease and when iguanas make love, when ice melts at will and over-proof babash cracks glass on window sills. Dry season sandy nose drips and dribbles snat through sub and superterranean ravines. Sewer cream, panty wash, ox swill, cock blood and natural gas. Pluric mist clings to the solid chrome stilts of shoreline shacks and doors are left open like wounds. Swelter from the firesky burns dust and excess oxygen causes cuss words to spark flames in the salty gust

—just flew up and into dust. Hot so hot even thumbtacks moan. Here sun cuts wax in a single glance, crisps lips stiff between syllables and cracks tongues like parchment in this heat haze, strong enough to churn thermo-carbines in the mountain tops.

Pious Auntie Mavis, Yoruba bone. Deaf in one eye. Kneading cornmeal in a long white robe, shredding saltfish in a one room asbestos bush shack overlooking Toucan bay, peeping through the luminous mist that engulfs the peninsulas. Her man Mr. Scipio stretched asleep in ergonomic flotation snores like a hacksaw blade. Three manfowl fight for the scraps of skin she throws out her window. Her window holds no glass, so the sea blows up from the horizon. Sunlight is crystallised through the shimmering leaves of a grugru bèf tree in her yard. Copper-beaked hawks know her papaya tree is pregnant. Each morning she throws rancid urine in the root.

She rubs soft candle in her navel, olive oil between her breasts, wraps her head white with calico cotton, binds her gown at the waist with red fisherman's twine. Salt over a shoulder. She lights her chillum pipe and adjusts her suncutter's brim. Humming hymns she packs her basket.

"Jesu, lover of my soul,
let me to thy bosom fly . . . "

She comin' down! Dress hem shaking shorter at the back, two baskets full, and leaves the kitchen door swinging. She sells ice, melon by the slice, chicken foot souse and coconut water, joy juice, sapodilla wine and turtle toe soup in Toucan Bay central market.

She fans her feet with a chicken-hawk feather because blue fly buzz round her shinbone and she hides a cold and open wound there, a seeping sore from tripping in trance on the mercy seat. Her good arse overlap the stool.

Beneath her sandaled feet, deep in pale-folk underground dwellings, sister Cynthia draws a mountain, sister draws a shack with two windows, an open door. Inside, two full women are sitting at a kitchen table shelling pigeon peas.

MA DAPHNE: Y'know de big Baptist 'oman who does sell tam'rind ball an' souse an' ting down by de jetty? Ms Mavis. Ah hear she sorefoot start back to bleed molasses.

MS YVETTE: O gorm, an she done got cataract.

MA DAPHNE: Umm hmm, ah hear she does grind coconut with she teeth to make sugarcake dumpling.

MS YVETTE: But dis time dey go have to chop it off?

MA DAPHNE: But yes, they should, imagine she kneadin' flour and that so' foot start to bite she.

MS YVETTE: Umm hmm, is syphilis dat bitch have!

Ms Daphne laughs, rims back an' skulls, and peas fall from her crotch.

⁓

Old bone dry snowcone man Scipio wakes with his eyes closed. His shrunken head appends a grey long beard. He wears a worn crown of ancient dreadlocks, a grey/green dashiki and slack rubber slippers. But he vex like a whip 'cause the sun caught him sleeping this morning.

Make haste he rides his homemade snowcone cart

through the Plaza Marina. Make haste it built from old iron physics, with cannibalised parts of a sand jitney, gris gris bones and reels of second hand teeth. Under the seat Scipio got a RX10 motor with low ride pneumatics, flags and rusty bells ringing on the jalopy wheel. So was Scipio rode. The three plastic canisters on the back tray hold cinnamon, cashew and sorrel syrups. The maldjo wood trolley box on the front fender: blocks of live ice wrapped in brown crocus sacking.

Scipio sets his stall outside the seaport gate. And soon come two black coolie sweating for snowcone—indentured Dravidian stevedores—gaunt muscle wrap dem bone with heat and slack hair. All morn they suffer, hauling interplanetary cargo in the transit pool. Scipio shaves ice into two foam cups and pumps syrup full and condensed milk over, two straws, and notices the Indian's money hand is a snake scale palm.

Not so, not me. Me I 'fraid snake— . . . snake? Snake used to walk upright like man in Eden before he play in 'e arse and jahjah fock 'im up, make under 'e bellow yellow. Ginger for wine but me I is a man like drink plenty lime. Lime juice or gimme rum anytime. But wine, wine is for bullerman, sippin' dry wine with they leg cross, sipping red wine an' skinnin' teeth. Pink wine, rose wine, white wine, cherry wine, port and all dem arse.

crick
    crack!

But Scipio buck when he hear one say,

"So Joe Sam beat man like pan las'night eh? Crack three Abobo man eye. I hear he even bat Bo Nuggy clean! How he bust Bo gut and lef' him to bleed."

"But Joe take some good jook too y'know. We did even break a Vat 19 seal when we see Manuel puncture 'e gullet, we thought Joe did dead."

"Joe be the demon seed my friend, the lion for real. They say is fish head, drake neck and puna yam he does swallow whole. Like is really only spirit lash could hurt he so, he does smoke in church."

23

She Swam in Heaven

i leave on the edge of mango season.
fruit being born on a tree beside the ravine are yet too
    green to chew.
cats run in the sewer gut growing jaws that shred
    linoleum.
and chasing myths through the undergrowth.
a mother's breast · falls · within glimpses of my head
when i hear the splash i turn with a stare as bare as a knot
    in claustrophobic cedar.
        it shakes spires off /centre.
it makes fabricated timber howl in dim corners.
        it's a wound like a stitch in wood
whose volume is its entire size.
a red mango ·a ripe mango veah· the first of the season.

threatening to leave the island, the ship shifts a wide arc
with engines spinnin' gusts of fire. blue drops of light
map the runway. we speed, as if through a channel then
    rise,
straining against night. we fly over cane fields and
    swampland,
we see ribbons of smoke on the northern range, lamp light
    from squatter's shacks, a hunter's flambeau, the
    luminous city . . .
until all we can see
are specks of the many stars that fell to the island.
and most are still gleaming.
we fly over knotted jungles, the gulf, the sea . . .
the island fading to a peninsula,
to dust on polarised glass, to fragments of a dream then
    fade . . .
        to black . . . gone—
                head won't turn left enough to view her.
                                    gone.

in a dream i asked,
"do you think we can come back next year?" and she said,
    "Yes,
we very must, and this has already happened."
and i saw then, from the veranda of my mother's house in
    kandahar village,
how sunlight pours through leaves like water through a
    sieve
            :::: leaving sequins on the ground :::: in
                        ripples at my feet ::::
and the sound of the river running under. and the
    resonance of wood.
and i said, "let this too be the memory of water,

like the first time you came to this floating island.
like the first time you saw a hummingbird.
                              and called her
                                  ïerè"

24

The African Origins of UFOs

. . . they set off to walk back to Africa

Dry word

So bruised and whipped with the blood of thorns, I'm ready
    now
to step through the eye of the vortex. Fixing a mask, a
    wooden helmet,
Bay leaf skull plate and shake to loose them lazy bones,
put bells on this bamboo saxophone.

Ma Mara she whisper a word to protect me on this

starflight. Ceboletta X give me strength. Mara placed beads of siderite, obi seed and psychic nut in a glass, marigold yellow for spirit force, magnet root for clandestine theological exegesis. She crack bergamot and ylang ylang oil and a pale blue halo begin to buzz; absorbing and absolving, becoming a transparent mirror, transmuting and receiving in a synapse like spirit bass walking five note natural scales and liquid tonic triplet tones and flatted fifths that creeps in every slip of time in this room with a dense scope of feeling that rises through the palm branch roof to some apex of red umbilical light where the sun sketched its arc · noon · blue has no skeleton. Carambola: no shell, calling or in flesh indistinct.

The source of this light is high above hills ·indistinct· a hovering something shifting improbable angles on the sky lid. It seems to transverse parallax and tremor in the stiff breeze, to shiver in the yellow Poui tree. When Mara falls she collapses between breast and shoulder. And her water tumbles. And her kidney fails, and she falls spinning
    spinning
    spinning . . .

Mother Mara, brown the hue of sunburnt clay, her word ablaze with liquid text, her eyes with ancient suns. Women of the village consulted her for the moon. Even Loa sought the solace of her brow. She blessed blades and bows and brewed herbal fetishes. In exchange the conqueros would bring her baskets of ripe corn, wild coffee, Sabicu seed and Iguana meat. They made sure her ground was pressed flat. And gave her secrets for safekeeping.

Their children call her Maman of many names. She is the great goddess who eyes shine like stars—ma ye ma ya ma ra ash ma i-sis—mother Mara who sleeps in the sky but remembers all our names.

She who construct the hologram.

Moist word

Hear nah. Dey send 'bout tutty man with plasma gun
an' jungle rat behine Daaga. But Daaga was a prince
y'know, six foot six an' bare muscle. Dem couldn' press he
so. An' when he spoke sound like carbide bust, cuss like
barber razor scraping sharpening strap. When Daaga burn
down de barracks an' jus' take he freedom, de bossman say,
"O jeez an'ages! He must be caught! He must not reach
the ocean, he may leave the island. An' anywhere he plant
that melocyte seed blacknuss sure to spread."

But Daaga did always say he would reach home, even if
he had to walk back to Africa. A man like he would never
submit to no bullwork—he too big for licks. Dey try pierce
Daaga heart with overwork and rumours of wounds but he
never blinkt. Dey send he alone to deep sea mine but he
never weep. Dey try crack Daaga soul with de cat-o-nine but
he never moan. Then one day he jus' peep a glimpse a free
an' is run Daaga run. He run 'cross de orange field, he run
through the rainforest barefeet—sideways east an' every
precipice he climb he look back. Picka jook 'im, bush bite.
Every crease an' every nook he scrape he wipe tracks.

Mara did know Daaga was coming. She vinegar tree
musta tell she dat morning. She gi'him crack corn an'
cassava bread. She prepare a balm for him, rub palm and

sole. She go inscribe sign in white chalk on a dirt floor altar and sprinkle asafetida in de four corners of her hut.

Dey say was like fire capsize in de sky when Daaga slip through the ruse. An' when Daaga mount de atmosphere, people run to peep from under dey jalousie to see de vessel rise. An' next day talk spread like leg round de island; from El Pena Blanca to Los Iros, how de ting shift light and fly, Daaga at de chrome an' de antimatter pumpin'!

Long time people used to call dem flying saucer, UFO an' space ship. Dey didn't know then 'bout panspermic dust. Dey never get genetic flashback. Or spend nine nights on de mourning ground. But now we know different, how plenty time them object appear in de sky, was just Daaga and those he led, lost in space, drifting from place to place, still trying find where they come from.

Printed in the United Kingdom by
Lightning Source UK Ltd., Milton Keynes
140079UK00001B/28/A

9 781844 712724